VALLEY OF THE
B[illegible]AR

C. A. MARRIOTT

Van Molle Publishing

First published in Great Britain in 1998
by Van Molle Publishing.

This is a work of fiction and any resemblance between the characters in this book and real persons, living or dead, is purely coincidental.

ISBN 0 9526925 2 X

Van Molle Publishing
PO Box 29
Cardigan
Ceredigion, SA43 1YN

Printed in Wales by
CIT Printing Services, Haverfordwest, Pembs.

PROLOGUE

Rhodesia, 1973

The two car convoy sped along the Al, Salisbury to Chirundu highway.

In the first car, next to the African driver, sat Blackie Schwartz, a sound recordist and behind him, engrossed in sorting out various pieces of equipment piled around him, was his partner and cameraman, Bob Martin.

In the front of the second car, Daniel Mpofu, the cook and unofficial interpreter, was happily exchanging gossip with the driver whilst behind him sat his twelve year old son and the third member of the South African TV crew, Lisa Barnard.

Travelling through the undulating tree covered hills towards Chirundu, the cars rounded a bend giving the occupants a sudden, spectacular view of the wide, flat plain that was the Zambesi Valley.

As the cars wound down the escarpment, occasionally passing troops of baboons searching the roadside verges for scorpions or other morsels of food, the temperature inside and outside the car rose uncomfortably.

Reaching the airless valley floor, Lisa wound down her window as far as it would go and leaned out, hoping to gain a cooling breeze. It was a mistake. It felt as if she had stuck her head into a furnace and the searing heat hitting her face made her abruptly sit back in her seat.

The cars turned off the straight, smooth tarmac and began to bounce across the fierce corrugations of a dirt road. Attempting to read through her notes, Lisa let out an irritated sigh as the words jumped and blurred in front of her. She would be glad when this particular assignment was over. Two weeks interviewing in the various South African Police bases in Rhodesia counted, as far as she was concerned, as a punishment.

Lisa felt the bubble of resentment rise within her as it had done so many times since being ordered onto this assignment – a propaganda exercise, aimed at keeping the families at home reassured. It could just as effectively have been carried out by any 'wet behind the ears' reporter. After all, it didn't take much talent to grin into the camera and ask 'What is the food like?', 'How are they treating you here?', 'Is there a message you would like to send back to your folks?'.

It was such stupid, infantile reporting when there was such a golden opportunity to do some real in-depth pieces on the dangers facing both Rhodesia and South Africa. Frustratingly, she had been given no option on the matter.

'What a waste of my talent!', she fumed, sickeningly aware that a couple more bland interviews with 'the boys out in the bush' would destroy all her hard work to be taken seriously in the man's world of investigative, hard hitting journalism.

Now that, she bitterly concluded, was the real purpose behind her being sent on this inane assignment. Fast becoming a household name for her strong reporting on major topics, and for being a champion of women's equality issues in her native country, Lisa knew there were some powerful people who were watching her progress with alarm. She was sure an attempt was being made to side line her from the dangerous political arena to the safer one of consumer and home affairs which, as she was so often told by her patronising male colleagues, was a much more fitting place for a woman reporter. Her mouth set in a firm line. They didn't know Lisa Barnard! She was not about to give way that easily and four years working in the system had taught her to be tough as well as ambitious and determined.

She gave up trying to read and leaned forward, looking through the gap between the men in the front seats. They had dropped back a little from the front car to avoid the worst of the swirling dust, the recent light rain having made little difference to the state of the road. She relaxed back into her seat, giving a confident smile to the boy.

The convoy continued to bump its way through the flat Mopani woodland, crossing the Nyakasanga river, heading towards its final destination, the South African Police base by the great Zambesi river at Mana Pools.

Suddenly, without warning, the earth erupted with a roar and a brilliant flash. With an ear-shattering explosion, a thick acrid cloud of smoke enveloped the first car. The second, skidding to an emergency stop, managed by inches to avoid crashing into it, the driver rapidly reversing back a few yards before switching off his engine.

The reverberations of the explosion died away, leaving an unnatural silence to descend around the four startled occupants of the second car as they emerged, shaken but unharmed, from the vehicle. They huddled together and looked about them.

Appalled, their eyes gravitated to the smouldering tangled mass of metal littering the road in front of them. At first glance, the back end of the car appeared almost normal except for the shattered window but on closer inspection, it could be seen that the sides had rippled and torn themselves away from the roof that now sat askew from its proper position. More horrific to the on-lookers was the fact that the driver's section of the car had completely disappeared apart from a burnt wheel and a few pieces of jagged metal still attached to the buckled chassis. The front passenger side was also badly damaged, the door twisted and crumpled, hanging at a forty five degree angle from the body of the car whilst the bonnet and front fender lay in a tangled heap twenty yards in front of the shell. All around lay small pieces of metal and other smouldering debris and in the middle of this, Bob Martin, blood stained and with hands covering his ears, staggered about in confused circles. There was no sign of the driver and Blackie Schwartz's mutilated body could be seen trapped in the mangled wreckage.

Still too shocked to react, it took several long seconds before Lisa broke free of her stunned, trance-like state and made to move forward. As she did so, Daniel pushed her back.

"No, Miss, you stay."

Telling his son to remain too, he motioned to the driver to follow him. They walked towards the still dazed Bob Martin and were about to lead him back to the safety of the second car when they froze.

Lisa, seeing them stop, turned to look behind her. Up until that moment she had been too stunned to register any emotion but as she watched, she felt her throat constrict with fear and for the first time realised her own life was in danger.

She saw a group of men stealthily emerge from the bush on each side of the road. She counted. Four, five, seven, eight, her mind automatically taking in that they were wearing an assortment of battle fatigues with packs, pouches and bandoliers. She also noted the sullen, blank looks on their black faces and the alarming array of weaponry they carried.

Slowly, in silence, they encircled the beleaguered group. As they did so, the driver dropped his hold on Bob Martin, turned and ran past the smoking remains of the front car. One harsh word spoken by what appeared to be the leader of the gang, broke the silence. Instantly, four shots ran out. The driver arched his back, frantically clawing the air as he fell face down into the vehicle rutted road, a slow trickle of blood spreading across the dust.

The leader then motioned two of the men to look into the wreckage. A few curt words were exchanged and another shot rang out. Blackie Schwartz was dead.

The leading terrorist, distinguishable from the others only by the menacing air he seemed to generate around him, ignored Lisa and deliberately moved towards the frozen figure of Daniel and Bob Martin, still too stunned to fully comprehend what was happening.

Lisa, her breathing coming in rapid, short gasps and with ears still ringing from the impact of the exploding mine, watched and heard everything through muffled disbelief.

Bob Martin turned to Daniel and spoke, his voice hesitant as he frantically tried to get his brain into gear.

"Tell him....... Tell him we are civilians. Reporters. TV reporters. We are not armed."

Daniel shook his head nervously, never taking his eyes off the terrorist now standing impassively – feet planted firmly apart, arms folded across his chest and rifle slung from his shoulder – only inches away from his face.

"Tell him god-dammit!"

Daniel spoke in Shona. The terrorist's stony face turned to instant rage. He hit Daniel across the face with such force that the cook staggered back a few paces then, failing to steady himself, collapsed to the ground, blood steaming from his nose.

The terrorist yelled in utter contempt at the cowering body then motioned his orders with a quick flick of a hand.

Four men moved forward. Two, having given their

rifles to comrades, grabbed the now struggling Daniel and held him fast whilst the other two gunmen placed themselves one to the front and one to the back of him. Daniel's eyes rolled in terror as they released the bayonets fixed to the barrels of their AK's. They proceeded to slowly and deliberately stab at Daniel, first in the buttocks, thighs and groin then up his entire body, until Daniel's animal screams of pain, rising with each terrible wound inflicted upon him, reached a chilling crescendo then abruptly ceased. The two holding Daniel released their grip and his lifeless body crumpled to the ground.

Lisa, still watching in mute horror, instinctively held the sobbing boy protectively to her until Daniel's cries ceased. Now the silence that followed was almost more unnerving than the screams.

The leader, unmoved, once more issued curt orders to his men. They quickly and thoroughly ransacked the second car, taking out all that was useful to them before setting it alight. From seemingly no-where, several unarmed porters scrambled out from their hiding places beside the road and hurriedly repacked the additional baggage.

The three survivors were herded together. Still dazed by the events taking place, their hands were bound behind their backs and cord nooses placed around their necks. Each noose was taken up by a terrorist who immediately proceeded to roughly prod and shove the captives off the road and into the bush. They were anxious now to get away from the carnage lest the pall of smoke billowing up into the blue, cloudless sky had already been detected and a patrol or air reconnaissance plane sent out to investigate.

Within moments the group had melted into the surrounding bush, leaving only the burning wreckage and dead bodies to testify that they were ever there.

It had all taken less than ten minutes.

CHAPTER ONE

Chirundu Police Station on the banks of the Zambesi, Rhodesia's border with Zambia.

Russell Forester sat at his desk trying for the seventh time to add a set of figures and get the answer he wanted. How he hated doing the monthly Mess accounts! Just as he was adding together the last figures in a long column, a commotion out on the forecourt broke his concentration.

"Damn it!"

He threw his pen down on the desk in disgust and walked over to the window. With hands resting on hips and a scowl on his face, he looked out across the immaculately kept Parade Square bordered by whitewashed stones and perfectly raked gravel to where, on the far side, three Constables were noisily arguing with a group of local villagers. Russell ran his hand through his dark, cropped hair, the scowl deepening as he watched.

The argument seemed to be getting out of hand with both Constables and villagers jabbing at each other ever more viciously with each heated exchange. Russell, muttering obscenities under his breath, grabbed his cap from the desk, placing it firmly on his head so that his hazel eyes glinted out from under the slashed peak, which itself almost touched his long straight nose and reluctantly left the comfort of his air conditioned office.

The moment he set foot outside, his light grey uniform shirt went dark with perspiration as the intense, airless heat hit him. Russell could feel the sweat oozing out of his body. Even his knuckles showed beads of moisture and it did nothing to improve his temper. Half way towards the unruly mob, he thundered out.

"Constable Matinah! What's going on here?"

Hearing and seeing the angry young officer striding towards them, the group fell silent and moved back a little to reveal an ancient white haired African, wrapped only in a dirty, torn blanket, squatting between the legs of the men. He was painfully thin and, thought Russell, quite the most pathetic looking specimen he had ever encountered.

Constable Matinah waved towards the villagers.

"They found this old man stealing mealie cobs from their shambas, Sah."

Russell inwardly groaned. 'I don't believe it! All this bloody ballyhoo over a couple of mealies. Just how much could an old man like that steal?' He glowered at the crowd and spoke in a firm voice that suggested no further argument would be permitted.

"Right! Tell them we'll deal with it. They can go now."

But if Russell was hoping that his order would bring the matter to a quick conclusion, he was disappointed. The villagers with many wild gesticulations, immediately broke out into a another round of loud arguments with Constable Matinah.

"They want the old man jailed, Sah."

Russell's thin lips pursed in exasperation. Some days, it seemed, were destined to be nothing more than one long aggravation. Had these people any idea of the amount of paper work involved in prosecuting the old man? He eyed the group of protesting men in stony silence. It caused a lot of shuffling of feet and downcast eyes, but the villagers held their ground. They were not to be dissuaded.

"Very well. Tell them we'll take the necessary action but..." Russell deliberately enunciated his next words, his finger pointedly emphasising his lack of patience. "....but before they can return home, they will all have to give statements."

'That should teach the buggers to mess me around', he thought with a degree of satisfaction. With Constable Matinah's speed at the typewriter averaging one word a minute, it would take all day for the statements to be taken which would mean there would be no afternoon session, drinking Chibuku beer, in the shebeen for the men that day.

The group realising further argument would not be tolerated, reluctantly broke up into groups of twos and threes, to await the long process of statement taking.

Meanwhile Russell and Constable Matinah each took an arm of the frail old man and lifted him to his feet. He was nothing but skin and bone and they all but carried him towards the Charge Office.

"Right, Constable. You might as well leave him out in the shade of the verandah. I don't think he's likely to run off anywhere. Get some food down him and find out who he is. Then you can begin to take the statements."

"Sah!"

Russell returned to his own office. He helped himself to a cola from the fridge standing sentry at the end of the corridor, grateful for the feel of the cool, refreshing liquid as it passed down his throat. He felt better. Tall and in his mid-twenties, he had the lean, tanned body of an enthusiastic athlete. However, during his six months at Chirundu – the aptly nick-named 'plug hole of the British Empire' – there had been very little opportunity to indulge in any kind of sporting activity, unless being commandeered by his Commanding Officer, John Makesmith, to join him in his terrifying game of chance, counted as a game. Makesmith, much to the alarm of his subordinates, was in the habit of taking the station's patrol boat out into the middle of the river in order to bait the

Zambian border guards on the other side. They, in turn, inevitably responded by firing live rounds back. Worse still for Russell was that, as a fellow Englishman, Makesmith expected him to join him in a display of fearless bravado by giving a robust rendition of 'Rule Britannia' as the bullets flew around them.

With a long drawn out sigh, Russell eased himself back into his chair to resume his calculations but it was not long before he was interrupted yet again. Constable Matinah stood in front of him.

"Sah! The old man has no relatives, all his family having died leaving no-one to look after him..."

"....So his village turfed him out to take his chances with the hyenas." Russell interjected.

Constable Matinah looked straight ahead and did not answer.

"All right Constable. Leave it with me." Constable Matinah left the room.

Russell leaned back in his chair and smiled at the incongruous picture of Elizabeth II, hanging on the wall. Somehow she had managed to escape the Republican axe after UDI – Makesmith's hand, Russell idly speculated – and so continued to regally watch over the comings and goings of the District Police Station. He rhythmically tapped his pen against the edge of the desk as he considered his options. There was no way he was going to prosecute a starving old man of seventy, or possibly even eighty years of age, over a couple of ears of corn! He made up his mind.

Leaving his desk, he picked up the Landrover's keys, telling the Duty Sergeant to sign him out for a couple of hours, before heading off towards the hills.

He drove down the main highway that eventually led to Salisbury and through the tsetse fly corridor, allowing himself to be directed into the large hanger by the Duty Tsetse Control Officer. Once his

Landrover was inside, the doors were closed and the vehicle sprayed with insecticide. A small window at the side of the building opened to draw the flies to the light – and to the waiting death trap. The wide land corridor was a cruel but necessary method of keeping the Tsetse fly from spreading onto the farm lands for the fly's habit of hitching a lift on the backs of animals, or indeed any moving object, ensured that any creature, large or small, found in the corridor, was shot. Russell had often listened in dismay to the hunters nightly radio reports to the Tsetse Fly Control Department listing the long and varied toll of animals shot. It was not a job he would have wanted.

Released from his temporary prison, Russell's mood changed for the better. The rough wooded bush on both sides of the tarmac road now changed to rolling fertile farmland. He drove on until, just before reaching the small farming town of Karoi, he turned off onto a dirt road which took him onto a private track leading to the beautiful old farmhouse of his friend, Franie Coetzee. Russell always felt a tinge of pleasure at seeing the first glimpse of the rambling white washed house, with its golden thatched roof, perfectly sited under the shade of a group of mature blue gum trees. It always looked so cool and inviting to the hot, weary traveller.

"Hello! Anyone at home?" Russell reached over to the back of the open topped Landrover and picked up a pack of beers.

"Russell! Well, this is a welcome surprise." The voice belonged to a tall, thin man of indiscernible years, grey and balding, who had come out from the shadow of the interior of the house to lean casually over the bougainvillea clad railings of the veranda.

"Brought some dumpies."

"Good boy. Come and sit down."

The two men sat and talked for a while, enjoying the

beer.

"Well, its always nice to see you, Russell, but I get the feeling that you came for a purpose. What can I do you for?"

Russell grimaced. "Am I that transparent? Well, Franie, I've come to ask a favour." He related the story of the old man. "So, I was wondering if you could find room for him here. I'm sure if I could find him a home, I could get him off with a caution."

"The poor old sod!"

Franie said nothing more for a while as he continued to drink his bottle of beer. Draining it, he lowered the bottle from his lips and wiped his mouth with the back of a hand blotched and spotted by years in the sun.

"Tell you what. You get him off the charge and he can come here. I'll make sure he gets fed and looked after."

"Thanks, Franie."

Franie merely shrugged as he flipped off the cap of another beer.

"Hell, we'll all get old one day. I'm relying on these black buggers to look after me when my time comes." He gave a short snort. "After all, how much can a skeleton like that eat?"

They fell into a companionable silence as they demolished the remaining beer but then Russell reluctantly rose from the comfort of the battered old wicker chair.

"Well, I guess I'd better be off. Can't sit here all day, much as I'd like to." His extended hand was warmly shaken by Franie. "The old boy will probably have to go before the Magistrate next week, then all being well, I'll bring him up. Thanks, again, Fran. I owe you a whisky next time we're both in town."

Feeling pleased, Russell jumped into the Landrover and raising a hand and a cloud of dust, headed back to

Chirundu Station.

The moment he threw his cap down on the desk, a deep voice boomed out impatiently from the end office.

"Is that you, Forester? In here. Now!"

Russell took a deep breath and walked into his Superior's office. He was greeted by the gaunt, unsmiling face of John Makesmith.

"Just what the hell do you think you are playing at?"

"Sir?"

"It seems, if I've understood the situation correctly, that you've suddenly taken to cavorting about the countryside finding homes for penniless Africans."

"Yes, Sir. Well, er, no Sir." Russell blurted, red-faced. "Just the one African, the old boy brought in this morning accused of stealing a few mealies."

"I see. And?"

"Well, I've just been down to see Franie Coetzee. He's agreed to take the old boy in, so I was hoping that if I can persuade the complainants to drop the charges, you might let the paper work go and I could take him up there tomorrow."

"Did you indeed." Makesmith threw down a pile of papers in undisguised irritation. Russell tensed, keeping his eyes centred on the polished brass catch of the window behind Makesmith's head.

"Russell." The tone seemed more conciliatory, "How many more times must I warn you about getting emotionally involved? Do I really have to remind you that you are a policeman not a bloody social worker? Your job is to uphold the law. That's it. Do you understand?"

"Sir!"

There was a long pause in which Russell's attention was momentarily distracted by the ache in his calf muscles as he continued to stand to attention. He therefore visibly jumped when Makesmith sprang his next biting accusation.

"So would you mind explaining to me what this complaint I've received from a..." Makesmith glanced down at the piece of paper in his hand, "...a Mr. Watts is all about?"

"Sir?"

"He says that you failed to take his burglary seriously and that you actually told him – and I quote – that you felt far too sorry for the burglar to apprehend him."

"Ah!" Russell, flinching under Makesmith's cold stare, cleared his throat.

"Well, Sir, I visited Mr. Watts's residence after he reported a burglary. On inspecting the scene of the crime, it was apparent that the burglar attempted to enter the house via the bathroom window which was situated above the toilet. In climbing through the window, the burglar put his foot down the lavatory pan and this was in such a disgustingly filthy state that I admit I did feel sorry for the poor bas – sorry, Sir – the burglar."

Russell saw an exasperated look cross his Chief's face and tried desperately hard to look more contrite.

"In all seriousness, Sir, I would like to point out that nothing was stolen, the burglar not surprisingly giving up at this point and as there were no witnesses, there wasn't a great deal more we could do. I therefore informed Mr. Watts that regrettably there was little chance of catching the culprit. It was then that Mr. Watts became abusive."

He paused and looked down at his feet before continuing.

"I admit that in replying, Sir, I did spell out a few home truths to Mr. Watts, which perhaps in hindsight I should have kept to myself."

John Makesmith looked so sternly at his young subordinate that Russell would have been very surprised to realise that his Superior was far less harsh in his thoughts than his outward appearance suggested. Indeed Russell so reminded him of himself twenty odd years before that it was impossible for Makesmith to pretend he didn't understand Russell's behaviour. Full of his own youthful ideals, he had left war scarred Britain in the early fifties, looking for adventure and success. It hadn't quite worked out the way he had planned, but then life very rarely did.

Having commanded the isolated station for the past ten years, Makesmith knew there were whispers in Salisbury that he had gone 'bush happy' – the diagnosis being based mainly on the fact that he ate only curry washed down with Lion lager and preferred the recorded speeches of Winston Churchill to the company of women – but it didn't worry him. Most of his colleagues had forgotten that there had been a woman once, but she had been unable to adjust to the dark continent and, homesick, had left him after six nervous, tearful months to return to a two up two down terrace in Manchester, taking everything with her except his prized record collection. Technically, they were still man and wife, but Makesmith had not heard from her for seventeen years. The experience had left him morose, spiky, generally antagonistic towards women. Chirundu was perfect for him. Men only and plenty of time to wander the bush in solitary conversation with himself. If that was being bush happy, he reasoned, then so be it. He had a station to run and let no man accuse him of not running a tight ship. He took pride in the efficiency of the station and now with the terrorist war, his little backwater was becoming more and more important as a front line defence against infiltration.

Makesmith squared his shoulders. Although he would never say so directly, he had a high opinion of his young Patrol Officer. Forester was good at his job, reliable and trustworthy, the sort of officer that was increasingly in short supply. There was therefore little point in over doing things. He relented.

"All right, we'll let it go this time, but... " he wagged his finger at Russell, "... you've had your last warning. Get your act together. You're a policeman. You don't judge and you don't get involved. Right!"

"Yes, Sir." Russell exhaled slowly and allowed the tension to ebb from his body.

Makesmith's tight lips moved in an almost imperceptible curve upwards that for him passed as a smile, and waved Russell to sit down.

"Right, then, on to more important matters. I want you out on foot patrol, leaving in two days time. Take Alistair, Constable Banga and Tracker Mazi with you. You're to patrol this area here." Makesmith pointed to the huge map pinned to the wall that covered their area of responsibility along the Zambesi, from the Kariba Gorge to the Mupata Gorge, going inland in a block some fifty miles deep. "We've received intelligence that a large group of terrorists are planning to cross the Zambesi somewhere in the Chewore area. You're to start your patrol there and work your way back along the river to see if you can intercept any spoor. I reckon it should take you three days. The helicopter will be ready to leave the South African Base at 0600 hours. Now remember, if you do come across any signs of infiltration, don't be a bloody fool. Keep your heads down and radio in for further orders and back-up. No heroics. Understood?"

Russell nodded, his mind already methodically working out what he would need for the patrol as he abstractly watched Makesmith sit at his desk and finish typing his patrol orders. Removing them from the machine, Makesmith checked and signed the papers then handed Russell his copy before dismissing him.

‘Oh well, beats doing Mess Accounts.’ Russell mused as he scanned the detail of his orders. He happily pushed the accounts to one side of his desk but as he did so, the deep voice from the end office boomed out again.

“By the way, Russell, I don’t seem to have had the Mess Accounts yet. They’re late. You’d better make sure they are on my desk before you go tonight.”

Russell glowered towards Makesmith’s office and pulled back the Mess file.

“Yes, Sir!”

CHAPTER TWO

By 0600 hours two days later, Russell, fellow Patrol Officer, Alistair Briggs, Constable Banga and Tracker Mazi were waiting on the helicopter pad at the South African base, some one hundred and fifty yards down the hill from their own Mess. Each was dressed in camouflage and festooned with equipment attached to their webbing. They carried four days food supply, ground sheet, water bottles, ammunition, FN rifles for the two Patrol Officers and a Greener shotgun for the Constable. Tracker Mazi remained unarmed. In addition, they would take it in turn to carry the large 28lb single side band radio now resting on the ground between their feet.

A clattering sound was heard in the distance and from the West a small dot appeared, growing bigger as the noise got louder. The Alouette helicopter flew low and fast over the tree tops towards the waiting group. It had come from the South African Base at Kariba whose helicopters serviced its three fortified sister bases that were strategically placed along this section of the Zambesi River Valley. The Alouette flared then landed, its South African pilot roaring cheerily out of the stripped down machine as it touched down.

"Right, so you're the idiots that volunteered for a quick spin this morning are you?"

The jovial jibe was a waste of energy on the part of the pilot. Nothing could be heard above the roar of the engine and in any event the four men were far too busy struggling to hold onto their hats whilst gathering up their equipment to notice he had spoken. Squinting against the blinding, swirling dust created by the slashing rotor wash, the three Rhodesian Policemen and their tracker threw their kit and themselves into the helicopter. As soon as the last foot had left the ground, the pilot gunned the engine and lifted the helicopter off the pad, immediately banking it sharply to his left causing everyone to leave their stomachs behind and Tracker Mazi to wail in terror. He never liked travelling in this giant and demented dragon-fly of a machine. He never trusted it or felt safe in it and was sure that the spirits disapproved of such a contraption. Not for the first time was he left wondering why the Europeans put such great store in being able to do such strange and unnatural things.

With a chuckle and a wry glance at his observer, the pilot steadied the helicopter, dipped its nose and scudded away across the tree tops. Russell looked out of the open doorway, viewing the imposing landscape spread out below him with real pleasure. This was always a part of the patrol he could unreservedly enjoy.

The rains had not yet arrived in force but showers had passed over the land, allowing a new flush of green growth to appear. Scattering into the dense mopani woodland to get away from the helicopter's rotor wash, he could see herds of elephants along with roan and sable antelope, impalas and his favourites, a family of wart-hogs whose line of stiffly erect tails he likened to the aerials on a patrol of little squad cars. He smiled secretly to himself as the helicopter sped on.

Twenty minutes after setting off, they reached the drop off point. The pilot swung the helicopter in a wide arc over the Zambesi and came round to a large area of grassland. There was no laughter from him now but deep concentration. He brought his machine to a hover ten feet from the ground. In an operational area, he had no intention of landing or cutting off his engine.

Satisfied with his position, he nodded to his observer who tapped Russell on the shoulder then indicated down with his thumb.

They baled out one after another, dropping their kit

to the ground as they jumped. Crouching down they spread out to form a defensive circle. Russell checked that the other three were out and clear of the helicopter then gave the watching crewman the thumbs up. Without further delay the helicopter moved off, quickly becoming a mere dot on the sky's horizon, the sound of its engine dying away, allowing the multitude of buzzing insects to re-establish themselves as the dominant sound to be heard.

Russell motioned to the others that it was time to move. They rapidly left the area but when they were sure they had safely put enough distance between themselves and the drop zone, they stopped for a brew up.

Sipping the sweet, welcome tea, Russell spread the map out before him. "Okay. We are here and it should take us about a day's march to get to the mouth of the Mupata Gorge and the Chewore River. From there, we'll turn inland, and follow the river." He carefully folded the map. "With the rains starting, I reckon we'll have our work cut out finding any spoor before it gets washed away. Right, everyone ready? Lets go."

The patrol moved off, feeling the effects of the increasing heat as the morning wore on. They came out of the woodland into an area of open grassland where a large herd of buffalo were grazing. As the men silently walked passed, only twenty or thirty yards away from the huge bulls standing guard on the outer edge of the herd, the animals stopped grazing and watched. There was no sound or movement from them beyond the swishing of tails and occasional flicking of ears as the oxpeckers, unconcerned, continued in their mutually beneficial activity of ridding the buffalo of unwanted ticks. From somewhere in the herd a buffalo snorted and in perfect unison, the whole herd turned and galloped away raising a cloud of startled oxpeckers and white cattle egrets who flew in indignant circles above the herd, waiting for their hosts to resettle. Russell felt the ground vibrate under the impact of their hooves. The buffalo stopped at the far side of the vlei, turned and once more studied the interlopers. The big bulls continued to stand their ground between the men and the herd, their heads held high, accentuating their massive bossed horns, until they were sure that there was no threat. Then, satisfied, they turned and re-joined their companions.

Russell gazed upon the scene with admiration. Wildlife had always been a passion of his and it was one of the main reasons why he had wanted to be posted to the district police. It was a thrill to him to be able to walk in the Zambesi Valley where, because of the tsetse fly, human interference was minimal. He fancied that he was sharing a similar experience to that which the early explorers must have encountered when they first entered the dark continent.

However, despite the lack of hunting in the area, the wildlife rarely showed itself, disappearing quickly into hiding as soon as it caught the scent of humans. There was always the electric humming of cicadas to be heard and it was not unusual to see flocks of lovebirds or, by the river, vivid scarlet carmine bee-eaters. Ungainly hornbills could sometimes be seen staggering from tree to tree and occasionally, iridescent rollers could be glimpsed as they darted out from cover to hawk insects. Insects... there were always plenty of those and it could be guaranteed that by the time the patrol was over, each man would have his fair share of red, blotchy bites courtesy of the tsetse fly and mosquitoes.

By mid-day, the ground had heated up to such an extent that Russell felt his face burning from the reflected heat coming off the dusty grey earth. The four men, Tracker Mazi in front, Russell, Constable

Banga and Alistair at the rear, walked, heads bowed, their arms and rifles resting across their ammunition pouches, the heat numbing their senses.

Russell trudged along, eyes unfocussed on the ground when some inner sense made him look up. Instantly he became alert and clicked his fingers. Hearing the warning, Tracker Mazi immediately stopped and lifted his own head, to see only yards ahead of him, two grey hulks emerging silently from the bush. The bull elephants, catching human scent on the wind at the same time, turned, raising their short tails in alarm whilst their trunks tested the air. Russell slowly and carefully took out one of his spare magazines and tapped it against his rifle making a metallic chunk, chunk, chunk noise. The elephants, ears flapping, trumpeted loudly but turned and shaking their massive heads, deftly merged back into the trees. They had no wish for confrontation.

"Wake up Mazi! A couple more steps and you would have barrelled straight into them."

"Sah! But it was because I was looking at the ground so hard. I can't see spoor looking up."

Alistair scoffed.

"More likely to have been in a stupefied daydream like the rest of us. Keep more alert in the future, Mazi, you're the one that's supposed to warn us of danger."

"Sah!"

The patrol continued through the exhausting heat of the day until just after three in the afternoon, when they made camp.

Russell organising the cooking stove was immediately handed a ration of corn beef and tinned vegetables by Alistair.

"Tell you what, Russ, you start the stew and I'll do the radio schedule." Before Russell could argue, Alistair quickly pulled the heavy, powerful radio to one side and erected the fifteen foot antenna.

"218, 218, this is 3.2.Alpha." Silence.

"218, 218, this is 3.2.Alpha." Continued silence.

Alistair swore. "Bet you anything you like bloody Madudzi is chatting in the Charge Office instead of being at his radio." He shifted his large frame and tried again.

"218, 218, this is 3.2.Alpha. Do you read me?"

Crackling was heard then, "3.2.Alpha, 3.2.Alpha, this is 218. I read you strenght five. Do you have any reports? What is your position. Over."

"218—3.2.Alpha. Negative. Nothing to report. Stand by for our position." The coded co-ordinates given, Alistair closed the transmission down by saying they would make contact again on the next radio schedule at 0600 the next day.

"Roger." Sergeant Madudzi acknowledged and the crackling came back.

Alistair switched the radio off. "Well, nice to know that we've been missed! How's that stew coming on, Russ, I'm starved."

Russell laughed. "Nearly done. Hey Banga, Mazi! Prepared to exchange some of your sadsza for stew?"

Once the daylight had gone, the small group moved off some hundred and fifty yards further inland to a patch of thick bush they had reconnoitred earlier as a nightly precaution against the possibility that their presence might have been detected from the Zambian side and a night attack attempted.

They spread their ground sheets making sure they had a tree at their heads and kit at their feet as protection against marauding hyenas, one of the biggest dangers to man in the bush. Settling, they attempted to ignore the common noises around them, made dramatic by the dark. Echoing cries from the bush babies and tree hyraxes competed with the chattering of the baboons and monkeys as they established their roosts and each man tried to banish any thoughts about the possibility of lions or, worse, opportunist hyenas coming into the sleeping camp to take a bite out of them. It was not uncommon to see an African with a large chunk of face or foot missing the damage having been inflicted by an hyena. Russell lay listening to the honking grunts of the hippos as they made their frequent roll call along the length of the river and wondered, as he always did on the first night out on patrol, whether he would ever get to sleep ....

He was awoken by a sharp pain in his side. It was caused by Alistair's size 12 boot digging into his ribs.

"Hey, come on man, it's time to move."

Russell grabbed Alistair's ankle as he made to make another dig.

"Okay, okay. You've made your point!"

He rose, stretching his stiff joints and took a deep breath of the cool dawn air. The heat had yet to take over and there was still a coating of dew on the ground. It was for him a magical time of day, giving him a tremendous feeling of rebirth.

After a quick breakfast of porridge made with Pronutro high protein meal, powdered milk and cold water, Russell radioed in his morning call to the Station, fully expecting nothing more than the usual mild irritation at finding Madudzi up to his normal behaviour – absent when required. To his surprise, Madudzi answered immediately stating that 'Sunray' wanted to speak with him. Russell raised his eyebrow at Alistair who stopped packing his ground sheet and moved over to listen. Only when something important occurred did the Member in Charge come on the air. They waited in anticipation.

"Good morning, Forester." crackled the unmistakable clipped tones of Makesmith. "We have had a major incident here. Yesterday afternoon, a two car convoy, containing a film crew from a South

African TV company hit a mine on the way out to Mana Pools. Some bodies were found at the scene but it appears that two whites, a man and a woman, are missing, presumed taken prisoner. There is also the possibility of a young African boy being with them as well. The spoor has been wiped out but the supposed terrorist group will now undoubtedly try and make it back to the Zambesi. We put stop lines of men along the river last night but so far there is nothing to report. Instead of proceeding on your original patrol, I now want you to return west along the river towards Chewore South African Police Base and see if you can spot any trace of the group. Numbers unknown but from indications at the scene, thought to be between ten and fourteen."

Russell acknowledged the changed orders and closed the radio down. Alistair already had the map out. They were at least fifty miles from where the incident took place, but with Intelligence suggesting that the terrorists had not gone in a direct line to the Zambesi but rather travelled diagonally across country, it could bring the gang up somewhere near yesterday's dropping zone.

Subdued, they silently gathered up their kit, both Russell and Alistair deep in their own thoughts, turning over in their minds the implications of this latest order. Without further delay, the small group started the long haul back, retracing the route they had travelled the day before.

The heat once more bore down on them as they trudged their way closer to the river bank, following a game trail through a large belt of tall grass and scrub. Russell, concentrating on shifting the bulky weight of the 'SSB' radio strapped to his chest, took a second to register that Tracker Mazi had sped past him shouting "Chipembere!".

He froze, scanning the bush ahead of him. He

heard the snort first, like an express train bearing down on them, then saw just above the top of the bush, the ears and horn of the rhino. Shouting a warning to Alistair and Banga, he crashed through the tall grass on his left and made towards some small trees. In one swift movement, he had dropped the radio at the base of the trunk and shinned up the first tree. As he watched the rhino pass by on the trail, Russell looked to see what had happened to the others. He spotted Alistair lying on the ground behind some rocks but then he saw disaster ahead. Banga had not moved, still standing, frozen, rooted to the spot, directly in the path of the oncoming rhino.

"Move, Banga! For Christ sake, move!" he bellowed but the figure of the Constable had been seen by the rhino. It accelerated, letting out loud, whooshing snorts as it dropped its head down to attack. Banga turned to run but it was too late. The horn of the rhino came up with a vicious jab, hooking deep into the body of the man and tossing him into the air. Banga let out a short, high pitched scream as he was lifted up and thrown through the air, arms flailing like a rag doll. He fell onto the grass some distance away as the rhino continued its charge. It seemed that the rhino was going to continue to thunder down the trail but then it suddenly skidded to a halt, turned, snorted and tested the air. Russell cautiously climbed down the tree and met up with Alistair. They held their rifles, ready to fire in case of a second charge, but the rhino merely snorted once more then turned and casually cantered off into the bush. As Russell put the safety catch back on the rifle, he was conscious of how violently his hands were shaking.

The two men hastened to the side of the motionless, broken body of the Constable. He was lying spread-eagled and unconscious in a spreading pool of his own blood, a massive gaping hole showing from his back to his chest. As they knelt there, knowing there was nothing they could do, they heard a gurgle and then the death rattle in Banga's throat.

"Shit Russ! The poor bastard. It was so bloody quick!"

Russell looked at his ashen faced colleague.

"There was nothing we could have done."

"But maybe if I had been quicker off the mark, I could have drilled the rhino before it reached Banga."

"There's no point in talking like that. There wasn't time and Banga should have moved. I can't understand why he froze. It's not as if this is the first time he's been out on patrol." Russell looked about him.

"Where's Mazi?" The two men called out but there was no reply. Russell cleared his throat and spat at the ground in a futile gesture of exasperation. He cursed.

"Bloody tracker!"

"He'll be back."

"Yeah, but when! Anyway, we'd better call the Station." He walked back to retrieve the radio from the base of the tree. Returning to the body, he crouched down and set the radio up.

"Madudzi had better be there!" He took three deep breaths to calm the thumping in his chest.

"218, 218, this is 3.2.Alpha."

There was an immediate response.

"3.2.Alpha, this is 218. Go ahead."

"Roger, Sergeant. Give me Sunray or Duty P/O."

A pause then the voice of the Second in Command.

"3.2.Alpha. Go."

"Roger. We have had a fatal incident here. A rhino has charged us and Constable Banga has been killed. Inform Sunray please. Stand by, I will give you our shackle coded position." Russell studied the map held by Alistair. He noted that Alistair's hands were no more steady than his own.

"Roger, 3.2.Alpha. Position noted. Assume rest of you okay. Stay where you are. We are sending a truck out immediately."

Russell signed off but left the radio on listening watch in case anything more was required. He looked at the dead body. The flies had already started to gather in their hundreds. It was hard to believe he thought, as he and Alistair carefully covered the body in a ground sheet, that ten minutes before Banga had been alive. The incident typified both what he loved and hated about Africa. He loved the unexpected, the sudden danger that came out of nowhere sending a rush of adrenalin through the body, the taste of fear and the exultation when danger had been overcome. Except for times like this when the danger had won. Then he hated Africa. Now there was a widow and two fatherless children back at Banga's home kraal.

The two men sat by the body, making notes. Both suffered feelings of guilt that they had survived and Banga had not.

Alistair finished his writing and studied the shroud covered body.

"You know he was a bloody good Constable. We can't afford to lose men like him."

"You can say that again. He could certainly be relied upon in times of trouble. I can testify to that!"

"Oh?"

"Yeah, last Rhodes and Founders holiday weekend, P/O Kelly and I got called to the bar at Makuti Motel. There was a messy fight in progress. Half a dozen yobs from Salisbury. When I called for quiet, the whole lot went to turn on me. I looked for Kelly – who I thought was standing behind me – but he had legged it out the door."

"What! Hell, man, that's not on. Not on at all!"

Russell gave a sour laugh.

"Tell me about it! Can't say I was sorry when he

got transferred to Mtoko. They're welcome to him. Anyway, there I was facing these drunken yobs, all baying for blood, thinking to myself, 'Shit, Forester, this is it, you're really for it this time', when Banga and two other Constables appeared beside me with thumping great big pick axe handles. Don't know where the hell they got them from, but it did the trick. Everyone became amazingly co-operative, we got the two main culprits into the truck and the rest of the drunken party just faded into the night. I tell you, Alistair, there are times when I think our black policemen are worth their weight in gold!"

"I suppose .."

A noise from the bushes stopped Alistair and had the two men tense and listening, simultaneously swivelling their rifles towards the sound.

"Don't shoot, Sah! Its me." Tracker Mazi's anxious face appeared from behind a tussock of grass. He walked over to the body of his comrade, lifted the ground sheet, studied the body then slowly shook his head from side to side, clicking his tongue.

"This is bad, Sah, very, very bad. He was a good man. Now who will tell the Widow Banga?"

"That's all being taken care of, Mazi. Where the hell have you been?"

Mazi ignoring the question, clicked his tongue a few more times before dropping the sheet back over Banga and settling himself down against a tree.

Watching him, it seemed to Russell that Mazi, like so many Africans, had a remarkable ability to accept death. He supposed it was because the tribal Africans constantly lived with such a thin line between life and death, but it was an outlook which he knew many Europeans mistook for a callous attitude towards the value of life itself.

After an hour's silence, Alistair turned to Mazi.

"Hey, you'd better go up by the river track and wait

for the transport to arrive, then you can direct it across to us."

Mazi slipped away. Left to themselves, the two Europeans exchanged desultory conversation as they waited. After several hours, Alistair sat upright.

"Hey, I think I hear something."

Russell strained to hear. After a few minutes his ears caught the faint whine of a straining engine heading in their direction.

The mine-proof vehicle, a strange mongrel with a Landrover chassis and an armoured bucket fixed on top with roll bars, threaded its way carefully between the trees and came to a halt nearby. P/O Johnson and two Constables jumped out of the truck and as they did so, a second Landrover pulled up behind. The Second in Command got out from the passenger side.

"Afternoon guys." He called. "You okay? Climb aboard the truck. We'll take it from here." With great efficiency, the area was mapped, measured and written up before the body was placed in an aluminium body box and everything packed back into the truck. Within half an hour it was all finished and the long, rough drive back to Chirundu had begun.

The journey back was made even more sombre for Russell as the truck thundered past the charred remains of a vehicle pushed clear to one side of the Mana Pools road. He realised it was the remains of the mine attack on the South African TV crew and shuddered. As the wreckage faded into the distance behind them, Russell forced his mind away from dwelling on the event that so closely mirrored his own private recurring nightmare.

Safely back at the Station, Russell and Alistair sat down to type out their reports on the patrol that had culminated in the tragic death of Banga, then handed them to the waiting Makesmith. He read them and satisfied, moved the briefing on.

‘Heartless shit.’ thought Russell as he listened to Makesmith’s brief utterances about the regrettable incident, but he had no time to dwell on his superior’s lack of feeling as he was forced to concentrate on what was now being said.

“There has been a degree of alarm following the mine incident at Mana Pools. As you know, up until then that road had been considered reasonably safe to travel. It now seems that our original assumption that the attack was undertaken by the group of terrorists we were expecting to cross over, is in fact incorrect. We have reason to believe that the large group crossing is still to take place, which leaves us with the question of just who did lay the mine and what have they done with the two missing South Africans. It is possible that it was carried out by a small group reported as being active in the tribal areas to the South and now presumed to be heading back towards the river.” Makesmith got up from his desk and moved towards the map on the wall.

“Tomorrow I want you to go back out again. You will start this side of your last drop off point and go along the Zambesi, towards Chewore and Mupata, where hopefully you will cut across one of the tracks, either the group crossing over or the group retreating.”

The briefing continued for a while longer, then dismissed, Russell and Alistair left the office and returned to the Mess. Russell stood under the hot, refreshing shower for a long time, as much to clear his mind of the day’s events as to revitalise his body.

‘We’d better organise a whip round in the Mess tonight.’ he concluded as he turned the tap from hot to cold.

CHAPTER THREE

At precisely 0600 hours the next morning, two Alouette helicopters left the Chirundu Station, heading out across the Zambesi Valley. One carried the patrol but the second was a so-called K-car, a helicopter fitted with heavy machine guns acting as a gun ship, the addition of which was a sure sign that the South Africans were nervous.

Russell's head echoed the thudding of the rotors. After eating a light meal the night before, he had paid a visit to the Mess Bar. Several other Policemen and a couple of Customs Officers were already there, drinking and playing darts but the news of Banga's death had caused the atmosphere to be subdued.

Deciding on a beer and an early night, Russell's plan had been diverted by the unexpected arrival of one of the local Game Wardens with three attractive young women draped on his arms. Their entrance caused an instantaneous electric silence to fall on the all male company who, to a man, sat open mouthed as they tried to take in the startling scene before them.

The Game Warden, hugely enjoying the impact of his entrance, had announced, by way of an introduction, that the girls were Australians, hitch-hiking around Africa. They had been 'collected' by him as they were heading for Kariba and persuaded by his devastating charm and wit – this utterance had occasioned the first real laugh of the evening – to divert to Chirundu for the night. Beaming at his success, he had escorted the girls to the long window seat before moving to the Bar to order the drinks. Within seconds he had been pushed aside as seven hitherto bored servicemen had found, in a rush of hormones, the use of their legs and voices. All had crowded around the girls, vying with each other as they attempted to impress the bemused visitors.

As the evening had progressed, and more and more beers consumed, the company had become overly rowdy with the girls treated to increasingly outrageous tales of heroic exploits. Then one of the Customs Officers, going out to the balcony to water the crown of thorn hedge below with the contents of his bladder, had instead found himself tipped over the railings by person or persons unknown.

Just who had played such a dastardly trick had then become a loud and all consuming argument between the Custom Officers and the Policemen as together they drunkenly tried to unhook the unfortunate man from the clutches of the poisonous thorns. When, finally, he had been freed, it was discovered that the Game Warden had taken the opportunity to sneak away, taking the three girls with him.

Since all had lost out, rivalry had been forgotten. With arms draped around each others shoulders, they had staggered back to the bar, consoling themselves with another beer and plans for revenge on the Game Warden next time he was foolish enough to show his face. Thus Russell had finally fallen into bed at one in the morning but, flat on his back, had then to deal with the sickening feeling that the entire room was spinning around. The problem had eventually been solved by resting his right foot on the floor which allowed him to fall into a fitful sleep until his batman woke him at five.

Bleary eyed, he ruefully regretted the folly of the previous night but by the time the helicopters had dropped the patrol, Russell's headache had reduced down to a nagging fuzziness which nevertheless persisted most of the day. He was secretly relieved that the day's patrol had proved so uneventful. He felt fragile and was in no mood for rapid thought or action.

Light rain had fallen in the night, forewarning the rise in the water levels that was to come but most of the rivers encountered during the day had been minor ones except the Chewore, and it was here that the patrol turned inland and made camp for the night.

Russell, deciding that it was time to commune with nature, took himself off a little way until he found a grass lined erosion gully ideal for his purpose. Using his sheath knife he dug a small cat hole then dropped his trousers. Squatting down, he let his mind go over the day's progress, or lack of it, but his reverie was interrupted by the growing sensation that he was being watched. He felt the hairs on the back of his neck stand up as he cautiously looked about him. He was almost at the bottom of the small drift, near to the edge of a muddy puddle that was all that remained of the rivulet. His eyes slowly moved down the gully, scanning the grass and rushes.

There, not eight feet away, a large face was staring intently at him. It was an hyena, but it so startled Russell that he let out an involuntary yell. Clumsily he attempted to stand up as with one hand he tried unsuccessfully to yank his trousers up from around his ankles and with the other, uselessly brandish his sheath knife at the bemused animal. To add insult to injury, as he stood up, he knocked over the one item of luxury he had brought with him – a roll of soft toilet paper. With no third hand to catch it, Russell could only curse under his breath as the priceless paper tumbled slowly into the water and with a soft plop turned to instant mush. The hyena, having no wish to confront the human, let out a cackle, turned and loped off but a different cackle had Russell sheepishly looking up. There above him stood Alistair, Mazi and Constable Chidziwa, Banga's replacement, all leaning on one another in fits of uncontrollable laughter.

"Hell, Russ, man, you let out such a blood curdling

scream there, I thought the 'terrs' had got you for sure!"

Russell glowered in bruised embarrassment. What an absolute idiot to have been caught out like that! The tale, with no doubt ever increasing embellishments would now do the rounds when they returned and it would probably haunt him wherever he went for the next six months! As it was the gales of laughter followed him as, trying to hang onto what little dignity he had left, he struggled up the gully and back to the camp. Late into the night he had to endure outbursts of smothered laughter as the other three re-told the sorry tale to each other. No amount of irritated demands for them to be quiet for safety's sake made any difference – it only brought on more bouts of sniggering. But finally the camp fell silent and slept.

They woke to another glorious African dawn. The air held a refreshing coolness that would soon be lost as the sun gained strength but for now, as the four men woke and stretched themselves awake, they relished the freshness that, judging by the exuberant morning symphony being sung around them, was equally appreciated by the birds.

Within half an hour the small group had brewed up and were on the march again, heading inland through open woodland, towards the escarpment some nine miles away. By eleven, they stopped for breakfast and called up the Station on the radio. They were not happy with the news relayed to them.

Special Branch had received information from their agents in Zambia that the terrorist gang had crossed the Zambesi during the past twenty four hours and the patrol digested this piece of information with some degree of alarm. Estimated to be twenty in number, porters would probably account for half of the gang numbers but that still left ten well armed and equipped fighters roaming the countryside. It also registered to the listening men that somewhere along the river line it was likely their paths must have crossed, so it was with a great deal more caution that they resumed their search. The patrol spread out, moving slowly and as silently as possible through the bush, listening with taunt nerves for the slightest sound.

For hours they continued their fruitless search, wilting under the effects of the ever present merciless sun. Russell, worn out with the heat and the tension that had stayed with them since their call to Chirundu, was just about to call a halt for the day when he saw Tracker Mazi, some ten yards ahead and to the right of him, kneel down. He held his breath. The other two also halted and looked towards Mazi. He beckoned Russell. There on the ground was a bootprint, or at least, a part of one. Russell let out a low whistle that brought Alistair and Chidziwa over to the spot. They carefully searched the area and found another bootprint, this time clearly imprinted in a small patch of muddy earth.

Russell and Alistair, with rising expectation, compared the print with the official spoor cards they carried which displayed all the different patterns of boot soles thought to be issued to the terrorists.

"That's it, man!" Alistair pronounced excitedly. "That's got to be it. No. 5, the star pattern."

"Yeah, I agree. Mazi, what do you think about the print?"

"Fresh, Sah. Very fresh. Today. Three or four hours maybe. No more."

The terrorists could be close, very close. Even watching them right at that moment. Russell felt a prickling sensation run down his spine and indicated to pull back into cover. The patrol retraced their steps for half a mile then, considering themselves to be reasonably safe from sudden attack, tucked themselves behind a large, ancient ant hill. Chidziwa was elected to keep watch. He wriggled to the top of the hillock that over the years had been rubbed down to a smooth hump by the thick hides of scratching elephants while Russell called up Chirundu on the radio.

"218, 218. This is 3.2.Alpha."

The call went unanswered. He tried again – and again.

"I don't believe it, that bloody idiot has buggered off somewhere!" His low voice was harsh with impotent rage.

"218, 218, this is 3.2.Alpha." No response. He gave up on 218. "Any station. Any station. 3.2.Alpha calling."

Instantly a female voice answered back.

"3.2.Alpha, this is 216. Can I help you?" It was Liz, the radio operator at District Head Quarters in Sinoia. Russell felt the relief wash over him as contact was made.

"Roger. I cannot raise station 218. Can you telephone and get someone to come up on the radio. We have an urgent situation here. Please notify Officer Commanding we have a potential follow up and contact situation and will require back-up."

Within three minutes, Makesmith was on the radio. Russell lost no time in venting his frustration over Madudzi.

"Request that Sergeant Madudzi be handcuffed to the radio whilst on duty. It doesn't do anything for our morale to be unable to make contact because he's gone walkabout from his post. We could be under attack here!"

"Roger." said the cool voice at the other end. "He will be dealt with. What is the real problem?"

Russell eased back.

"Roger. We have cut the spoor. Repeat. We have cut the spoor. They're moving towards the escarpment. Over"

"How fresh do you estimate the spoor to be? Over."

"Only three to four hours old. Request back-up. Over."

"Roger. Will arrange for Crusader or Pilgrim to join you. Stand by."

The four men on the ant hill waited for the reply, all hoping they would get Crusader, the call sign for their own Rhodesian Light Infantry. The radio crackled into life.

"3.2.Alpha?"

"218. Go."

"Have checked. Army not available. There is a large on-going operation at Mount Darwin and Centenary. We are calling in Pilgrim. Stand by."

"Oh, shit man, thats all we need, the bloody Slopes charging about all over the place!"

It was Alistair who spoke but it echoed Russell's thoughts exactly. Their opinion of the operational skills of the 'Slopes' – as the South Africans were nicknamed for their habit of hitting their foreheads with the heel of their hands and exclaiming "Oh God!" – was not high. Indeed the Rhodesians, trained under the harsh discipline of the old pre-war British Army manual, considered the South Africans to be nothing less than dangerously lax. The two black Rhodesians, detesting the South Africans, exchanged glances but said nothing.

The radio crackled into life again. Makesmith's voice came on the air.

"There is a force of Pilgrims enroute from Chewore base, numbering two zero, that is two zero men. Your position has been given and they will get as close as possible by truck then walk the rest of the way. Stay where you are. Repeat, stay where you are until they come to you. Estimated time of arrival, three hours."

"Roger. But it will be getting dark by then. If the

terrorists continue to push on through the night, we'll loose them."

"Your position understood. It is to be hoped that having been on the move for nearly twenty four hours, they decide to rest up before climbing the escarpment. In any event they should be moving more slowly than you. Rendezvous with Pilgrim, rest overnight and start follow-up operations at first light tomorrow."

"Roger."

"Stay on listening watch overnight – and Good Luck!"

Makesmith signed off and the four men settled down to wait once more. The worst part was not being able to have a cigarette for fear that the smoke might be detected. It was impossible to tell just how far ahead the terrorists might be. However, they risked brewing up a cup of tea on their small gas stove as they waited, the atmosphere of quiet tension filling the warm evening air.

As he sat and watched the sky above him subtly change its hue from bright day light blue to dusky evening purple, Russell wondered, not for the first time, how he had got himself into such a potentially dangerous situation. He certainly hadn't planned to become a mercenary, but now, caught up in somebody else's war, he sometimes felt that was what he had become. Worse still was the fact that he considered he was risking his life fighting a war the white Rhodesians couldn't win.

He let his mind roam back over the past couple of years of his life in a futile attempt to subjugate his craving for a drag on a cigarette. He had joined the BSAP as a way of getting back to Africa, his first home, Kenya, no longer being an option for him. At nineteen, his parents had insisted he go to London, convinced that there was no future for a white man in post colonial Kenya. In totally alien country, he had lasted three years in a City bank before the weather, the crowds and the tedium of his job had driven him to desperation. In a moment of weakness, one very cold and wet March morning, he had applied to his childhood heroes, the British South Africa Police and almost within days, an air ticket had been in his possession. Before Russell Henry Forester had time to reconsider, he was in the Training Depot, signed up, shaven headed, swearing the Oath of Allegiance. He had never looked back.

After the initial shock of the harsh training, Russell had found he relished the work, even its discipline becoming a source of pride to him. Once graduated, every day presented a different challenge from sorting out grisly road accidents to rendering first aid in remote villages. It was a job that gave him responsibility and a defined purpose rather than just pen pushing behind a desk and Russell thrived on it. The District Police also offered the best prize of all – an unrivalled opportunity to explore the bush. Indeed, he had on occasions patrolled to places so remote that his was the first white face the village children had ever seen.

But now he was restless. He knew he had matured a great deal since joining the force, two and a half years before and was grateful for the direction it had given him. But he also felt cheated that only months after he had left the training depot, the war of attrition had been declared, changing forever the way of life he wanted to live. Now his duties were as much about anti-terrorist fighting as it was with the recognised police role he had signed up to carry out.

Russell inhaled deeply, the scowl on his face indicating his profound agitation. Trust the black man to bugger up his democracy for a second time! He knew he was being unfair. He had seen it first hand in the Police where black sergeants with over twenty years experience were routinely ordered about by rude, ignorant white conscripts half their age. It made Russell cringe with embarrassment. Couldn't the Rhodesians see that they were going to loose it all if they didn't change?

He impatiently stubbed his toe against the hillock in a useless gesture of frustration. None of this rambling helped him decide on his future but with his three year contract expiring in six months, he would very shortly have to decide which way to jump. The problem was that as much as he loved the police role, the job he had signed up to do was no longer there, nor was it likely to be in the future. So where did that leave him? Between a rock and a hard place came the answer. Alien Britain or Black Rhodesia. Neither alternative appealed. His gloomy thoughts were cut short by Mazi.

"Sah, I hear something is coming."

They all strained to hear. At first, Russell could detect nothing beyond the first chirrups of the crickets and tree frogs warming up for their nightly concert, but then he heard the chink of metal. He slipped the safety catch off on his rifle, as did the other two and raising his head cautiously over the top of the ant hill, peered out into the gathering gloom towards the direction of the noise. If it was the terrorists paying them a visit, he thought, three against ten wouldn't be great odds in their favour. He swallowed, his mouth drying. The waiting seemed endless but then Mazi nodded out towards a tree to their right.

Russell squinted in concentration. There it was. A movement. A silhouette of a man between two trees. Now he could make out several other men edging slowly in a line towards them and resumed breathing. In the half light, he could just make out the pale camouflage fatigues of the South Africans. He gave out a low whistle and the advancing men froze.

"Hey! Pilgrim, this is Bailiff."

A strained voice called out in reply.

"Where are you?"

"Straight in front of you at the ant hill." Russell stood up and showed himself. The band of Pilgrims appeared through the bush, the tension easing on their faces as they joined the small camp. A tall, thick set man showing close cropped blond hair under his bush hat, came up to Russell and extended his hand.

"Lieutenant Viljoen. I'm the Commanding Officer at Chewore Camp. I've had to bring out most of my men. There's just a section left holding the fort so I don't want to be out too long."

'What a pratt!' was Russell's immediate thought but he shook hands and offered a smile.

"Understood. I'm Patrol Officer Forester, that's Patrol Officer Briggs over there and this is Constable Chidziwa and Tracker Mazi."

"Just the four of you?"

"Yes."

Lieutenant Viljoen was disgruntled at seeing such a small number and the look of dismay did not go unnoticed. Russell raised a silent eyebrow to Alistair but after the moment's hesitation, Lieutenant Viljoen shrugged resignedly.

"Okay.... I guess we're getting used to fighting your war for you. Where are the tracks?"

Russell ignored the dig and nodded behind the Lieutenant.

"About half a mile that way. We pulled back here for safety. We don't know how far ahead the terrorists are, or even if they'll make camp tonight but even so, we would suggest that its too dark now to do anything tonight."

Lieutenant Viljoen readily nodded his assent. He had no intention of crashing about the bush in the dark.

"Good." continued Russell, pleased that there would be no arguments. "Then if you agree, the best thing to do is to camp here and just hope to hell it doesn't rain overnight and wash the spoor away."

"That is what I was thinking myself. You can rest up now. My men will form the defensive perimeter. Where are your kaffirs sleeping?"

Russell bridled.

"We don't refer to them as 'kaffirs'. As fully attested members of the BSAP and part of our team they sleep right here, next to us." Seeing Viljoen open his mouth to complain, Russell, barely able to disguise his dislike of the man standing in front of him, acidly cut across any objections.

"They share our dangers, they share our camp. Okay?"

The Lieutenant was not happy. With a flick of his head, he pointed to the far side of the makeshift camp.

"Very well. In that case you had all better sleep over there." He drew a line on the ground with his boot. "We'll take this side." He curtly turned his back on Russell. To Viljoen, a policeman more accustomed to the Johannesburg suburbs, the bush was a dark, encroaching, hostile place where aggressive animals and biting insects plagued him night and day. He was not enjoying his three months posting as commander of a remote fort on the Zambesi but far worse for his peace of mind than the dangers of the bush was the terrifying possibility of the black man attacking him. What was there to say that the two blacks skulking in the far corner of the camp had not become infiltrators just waiting for the right moment to kill? With a wife and two year old waiting for him back home, he was taking no chances. Speaking in Afrikaans, Viljoen ordered his men to keep alert for any possible signs of danger – from inside as well as outside the camp and bedded down with as many of his men between him and the two Africans as he could reasonably manage.

Russell collected his gear and with Alistair joined Chidziwa and Mazi. Feeling the depth of their resentment towards the South Africans, Russell couldn't blame them, nor look them in the eye. All he could do was silently curse the arrogance of the Lieutenant. Tomorrow the brave Lieutenant would expect Chidziwa to fight along side him – and if necessary die for him – yet tonight he couldn't even share a camp site with him.

Somewhere in his sub-conscious, a thought process clicked into place and although the conclusion was not clearly formed, Russell knew that he would have to leave Rhodesia – and scotch any idea of moving down to South Africa. He couldn't go through this long drawn out independence struggle a third time.

Alistair settled himself down next to Russell and gave him a nudge in the ribs, talking in a low whisper.

"Did you see that look when Viljoen realised there was only four of us?"

"Yeah, had me thinking of that old joke, 'there we were, four against four thousand, the toughest four we ever fought'!"

Alistair let out a quiet chortle and slapped his forehead in a mock salute.

"Yoh Gott!....but heaven help us tomorrow." He turned over to sleep.

"Alistair?"

"What?"

"Do you ever wonder why our black policemen are so loyal to us, given the way they are treated?"

"Hey, Russ, man, that's far too profound for me. All I'm interested in is getting a good night's sleep."

"Sorry Al. Good night."

Russell smiled in the darkness as he heard an almost instant rhythmic breathing coming from Alistair but sleep eluded him.

He lay, listening to the unaccustomed sound of so many men around him. Looking up to the night sky, he surveyed the millions of staggeringly beautiful stars that arched over him, so distant and yet so bright it seemed he could reach out and touch them.

The sounds of the African night closed in around the camp but the whooping of the hyenas, the distant roar of a lion somewhere out in the darkness held no fear for him. They were the noises he expected to hear and he found them comforting.

It was the train of his own thoughts that day that unsettled Russell and made him apprehensive about what the following one might bring. The stars continued to sparkle serenely overhead as Russell contemplated the futility of worrying about his future when perhaps he didn't have one.

Tomorrow. Tomorrow might be the last day of his life, the day his luck ran out, the one with his number on it. After all, how many times could he drive over land mines where the detonators had been placed upside down and thus failed to explode or his tyre tracks be discovered just half an inch away from a live mine and disaster?

He tried being positive. The terrorists might be too far ahead for them to catch up. But on the other hand, his alter ego immediately challenged, the gang could be aware of them following and be setting up an ambush for them. The gloomy thoughts pervaded his mind.

He mentally ticked off all the incidents of near-misses he had survived. The time when an armed gang had hidden in the storeroom at the back of a duka, but because he had been too lazy to pick up his Uzi submachine gun from the passenger seat and had walked in unarmed, they had held back from firing. He turned cold now at the thought. How many more times in this conflict could he cheat death? Perhaps tomorrow ......

Despite his pessimistic thoughts, his mind, finally as tired as his body, drifted into sleep until in the pre-dawn light, one of the South African pickets woke him.

He became conscious of the ring of men around him taking up their weapons as they followed the dawn and dusk ritual of 'standing to', which according to the manual was the most likely time the enemy would attack. Russell dryly noted that it was just as well the terrorists did not seem to read the same manual for as soon as dawn broke, the order to 'stand down' was given and the men immediately put aside their weapons and concentrated on breakfast.

In the freshness of the dawn, all morbid thoughts went out of Russell's mind. The air was crisp, the dawn chorus was in full swing and nearby a group of impala were contentedly nibbling the dewy vegetation. It was a perfect start to the day.

Tracker Mazi set off to scout ahead whilst the rest brewed up a cup of tea. He came back to report that the spoor was still clearly visible. Their luck had held, it had not rained in the night.

The camp packed up and within half an hour, they arrived back at the spoor. The area was examined thoroughly by Lieutenant Viljoen and his men. It looked as if the gang were following an elephant trail that led to, then slowly, almost imperceptibly climbed to the top of the escarpment. The men spread out. Russell and Tracker Mazi took the lead, out on point. Alistair and Constable Chidziwa followed some fifty feet behind and to their left. The South Africans started to spread out in the bush, forming a loose double line, ten men wide. Slowly they methodically combed the area, wading through dew covered bushes that wrapped their legs and arms in glittering, clinging, gossamer spiders' webs.

The mopani woodland gave way to a large area of

grass with scattered trees. Conscious of the beauty of the place, Russell thought it gave the impression of being deliberately laid out like a country park. He stopped at the edge of the woodland and stared intently ahead.

The open land ran down to a small river at the bottom of a drift. The banks of the river were shrouded in bushes so that the water itself was obscured. The trail they were following continued out of the woodland, across the veld towards the river and beyond. If they were to follow, they had to cross the open ground to the river and risk being exposed with little cover. Russell weighed up the situation, then catching the eye of Lieutenant Viljoen, indicated that they were moving slowly across and down.

Viljoen gave a hand signal command to his men and Alistair gave him the thumbs up. Russell, adrenalin beginning to pump through his body, tapped Mazi on the shoulder and moved out into the open grassland. He felt extremely vulnerable, all too visible for comfort.

He and Mazi moved down towards the bushes at the river's edge following the spoor, a footprint and beside it, a rifle butt imprint so fresh that the Chinese characters on the plate were clearly discernible.

Suddenly, unbidden, he heard in his head the voice of Mukora, the old African, sitting talking to him as a child.

"Listen to the birds, they always tell you what is there."

The sticky sweat down his back turned cold as Russell's brain registered that all around him was still, no bird song or movement at all, just a heavy, all pervading silence. He extended his arm out and flagged Mazi, pushing his hand down towards the ground. Mazi nodded. They crouched down and moved more cautiously forward, eyes straining to catch any untoward movement ahead. Russell edged towards one of the lone trees that dotted the veld.

Almost simultaneously, there was the sound of gun fire and the bark of the tree erupted chippings into the air just above his head. Out of the corner of his eye, as he threw himself belly down in the grass, Russell saw Mazi drop flat as a pancake and rapidly snake off through the grass back towards the woodland. Unarmed, it was not his job to fight and he would disappear in the safest direction and hide until it was all over.

The burst of gunfire was definitely the high pitch stutter of an AK and it fired again in Russell's direction, showering him once more with chippings, branches and leaves. He was thankful that whoever was firing was shooting uphill and had obviously miss-judged his aim.

The stutter of the AKs was now matched by the boom of the FN rifles and the South African's light machine guns. Russell kept his head down, deciding to wait for the South Africans to safely pass him before raising himself up for, in this kind of situation, they had the reputation of shooting anything that moved. He did not have long to wait however before he felt the vibrations of their boots pounding the hard earth as they charged past him. Alistair was quickly at his side.

"You okay?"

"Yeah – just!"

"Thought they'd really nailed you that time." Alistair slapped Russell on the shoulder and was off. "See you later!"

Russell knelt up. He could see the disappearing backs of the South Africans as they ran into the scrub on the river's edge. He stood up, pulling the quick release handles on his pack, which left him with only his water bottles, ammunition and kidney pouch.

Everyone reached the river and crossed into

identical scrub on the other side. The South Africans were ahead, running, yelling, firing from the hip. As Russell came out of the water, he caught a glimpse of a man running slightly to the right of the main group. He followed.

The man was fast, running through the scrub land, jinking like a rabbit as Russell fired several shots. The man turned and aimed his AK at Russell who threw himself onto the ground, feeling the bullets whistle over his head. Looking up, he saw the man disappearing towards a rocky outcrop and tore after him heedless of the danger until, running past the rocks, he heard a movement beside him.

He froze in mid-stride and turned to his right. There was a gun pointing straight at his chest.

CHAPTER FOUR

Russell looked into the face of his antagonist. It was covered in beaded sweat but not in fear, the eyes holding Russell's without flinching. They stayed locked in the mutual stare for several seconds – to Russell it seemed an eternity as he waited for the trigger to be pulled. His eyes registered the slight change of expression in the man's face as the decision was made, saw the forward movement but could not react quickly enough to prevent the butt of the gun hitting him in the groin. Crying out in pain, his legs buckled as the man ran past him, back towards the river.

Crippled, it was several seconds before Russell could stand. Picking up his own rifle from where he had let it fall, he shook his head in disbelief. Then, irrationally angry at the man, he began to chase after him with a rashness that should have got him killed.

Crashing through the undergrowth, splashing wildly through the water, back up the far bank, Russell got his man in his sights. It spurred him on to greater effort. Closing the gap between them, he fired a couple of wild shots, missing the fast moving target but none the less causing his adversary to stumble and crash to the ground. Before he could recover, Russell had his rifle muzzle pushed into the back of the man's neck. Fighting to catch his own breath, Russell barked out his orders.

"You! Get up on your knees. Put your hands on your head. *NOW!*"

Russell moved a few paces to the side, allowing the man to obey the orders. Facing each other, the man, straight backed and proud, still looked unflinchingly at Russell. His eyes seemed to bore into Russell's mind so that Russell hesitated. He had to ask.

"Why didn't you kill me when you had the chance?"

The man nodded towards Russell's chest. Russell glanced down. The pendant he always wore around his neck was dangling in full view. It must have come free from his shirt in the fray. The man slowly moved his left hand down towards his own neck, checked as the barrel of Russell's rifle moved an inch closer, then continued to carefully pull out an exact replica.

"Whoever wears the amulet is a brother." The man let out a contemptuous laugh at the irony of it all. After all those brain washing lectures he had endured by his communist instructors against the idea of the existence of God, all the ridiculing he had suffered at their hands as they tried to rid him and his fellow African comrades of their belief in spirits and ancestors, and now, at the very first test, it had all counted for nothing. The spirits of the amulet had effortlessly controlled his movements without a struggle, even though it might result in his own death. He wasn't sure whether he was angry with himself for his weakness or relieved to discover that he had not, after all, been completely stripped of his soul. His face straightened and his voice became bitter. "Very stupid of me, of course, because you must have killed someone for yours!"

The accusation touched a raw nerve with Russell. "I certainly did not!" he protested, incensed. "I was given it by an old African when I was a boy in Kenya."

Two things went through Russell's mind. First, surprisingly, the man spoke English with almost no accent at all – there was just a slight imperfection that jarred and puzzled. The second thing to strike him was that after not having thought of him at all for several years, he had twice remembered Mukora in the space of less than one hour. He jerked his head towards the man.

"So how did you come by yours?"

The man still frowned at Russell. "It was my Father's and his Father's before that and his Father's before that.."

"...All right, all right, I get the picture. So you're claiming to be a descendant of one of the original two hundred Guardians?"

The man's face turned from anger to complete astonishment.

"You know of the Valley of the Black Spear?"

"The old man told me a story when he gave me this amulet, though I never really believed it."

Now it was the African's turn to look enraged. Having surrendered unconditionally back to the power of the Spirits, he snapped back in their defence. "But it is true! The history has been passed down from father to son with the giving of the amulet for generations and will continue to be until the day of restoration."

"Yes, yes, I've heard all that spiel before." Russell's dismissive tone angered the man.

"That is so typical of you whites. Just because it is not written down in a precious book, you think it is just made up stories to rubbish and dismiss!"

"Okay, okay. So. Tell me. Where is this fabled Valley?"

The man hesitated, a slight frown appearing on his face.

"I don't know. Not exactly." He saw the look of derision on Russell's face. It made him once more stiffen in pique.

"It is somewhere over there." He nodded his head in the general direction of Zambia.

"The original Kingdom of Zimbabwe stretched right up as far as the Great Lakes to the North. We are told that when it is time for us to return to the Valley, the Spirits will guide us to the right place. Until then the descendants of the two hundred must keep vigil and keep faith even though they are scattered across the length and breadth of Africa."

Russell, wiping the sweat from his face with his arms, gave a short grunt. This had to be the most ridiculous, improbable situation of all time. Here he was, holding a rifle to the head of an escaping terrorist and having a conversation about a long lost fable as if they were at a casual dinner party. But he acknowledged that he had placed himself in a dilemma.

However far fetched the story of a lost Kingdom might be, the amulet had undoubtedly saved his life. Any terrorist taken prisoner was automatically sentenced to death. Shooting, wounding, even killing someone in the frenzy of a fire fight was one thing, but having talked to this man, discovered some link, however tenuous, between them, made it difficult for him to order the man to walk back to the South African camp, the Rhodesian Special Branch and the certainty of being hanged.

The man, studying Russell intently, seemed aware of his plight. He cocked his head and after a pause, spoke again.

"You looking for a white man and woman abducted a few days ago ?"

"What if I am?"

"I know where they are being taken. We passed the gang – they are not part of ZAPU but a returning party of ZANLA – as we crossed the Zambesi. I know where they are resting up before crossing the mountains back to Mozambique. I could take you there and get you back across the Zambesi ...."

"... As long as you remain on the Zambian side." finished Russell dryly.

The man's shoulders rose in an all embracing shrug.

"Of course."

He should dismiss such a blatantly one sided plan immediately as nothing more than a wild escape attempt by the terrorist, but instead Russell found his mind racing through the possibilities. Go into Zambia? It was stupid. He had no radio to ask for back-up yet if they were to attempt a rescue operation, time was of the essence. If they waited, by the time the interrogators had finished with this man, it would be too late to do anything to help them. In any case, he acknowledged to himself, if the hostages were in Zambia, the Authorities would never mount a rescue operation into hostile territory. It would be tantamount to an act of war and cause Prime Minister Smith serious political problems he could well do without. No, an operation across the river was out of the question and alone, what could one man do?

His mind saw the vehicle being blown up, saw the woman being taken hostage, imagined her terror as the gun was placed to her head. But the face he saw was not that of the unknown South African but that of Sara. Deep in thought, he was unaware of his facial movements as his nightmare returned to haunt him in broad daylight. He remembered with a pain that made him wince, his beautiful, vivacious Sara. It had been planned that after finishing his three year contract, they would marry and live on her parents' farm which would then one day belong to them. It had all seemed perfect but then came the day her parents begged him to stop her going with friends on a trip to Beira. She had looked at him with her liquid brown eyes that willingly offered 'I'll stay if you want' but he had shrugged his shoulders. "If she wants to go....." and the following day he had sat opposite her distraught parents in the hospital, watching as her life ebbed away, blown away by a mine.

The pain was still there. The anger. The guilt that he had not stopped her. He was racked by indecision.

Was another woman going to die because he did nothing? Every sense in his head was telling him he should have nothing whatsoever to do with this crazy plan but perplexingly he found himself saying something different.

"How can I trust you? You could lead me straight into the arms of ZAPU or simply just leave me stranded on the opposite side of the river and disappear into the bush. It all sounds as if I'd be taking a tremendous bloody risk with you."

The man touched his amulet. "Those who wear the amulet are brothers, bound to each other by a force greater than life itself. If it was not so, you would already be dead."

It was a sobering thought for Russell. Could he really leave the safety of Rhodesia, all but desert his post, put his life in the hands of a terrorist, just to find a woman he did not know and who, more than likely, would by now be dead?

Russell studied the man, trying to get the measure of him. Even kneeling, it was clear that he was imposingly tall, probably taller than himself by at least three inches. He was well built but lithe, with a thin, intelligent face. The long narrow nose and thin lips made Russell think of the Masai in Kenya rather than the Southern tribes, but it was his eyes that held attention. Almost amber in colour they burned with a leopard's intensity. Now they held Russell in a penetrating gaze. He showed no sign of impatience, fear or worry. He just knelt there, hands together at the back of his head, waiting for Russell to make up his mind about both their fates.

From deep within him, Russell felt an overwhelming force well up, compelling him to go.

'Damn the man!' Russell's head began to throb.

"Go." said the force from within. It made no sense at all, but the word pounded in his head. "Go. *GO!*"

He slowly lowered his gun and clicked the safety catch over. The man now carefully let his arms down, allowing himself the luxury of a long, slow exhalation of breath.

"You say you know where the gang's taking the two white people?"

"Yes. There also appears to be a young boy. The woman looked dead on her feet, but they were all alive when we saw them. That was two nights ago."

"Then we'll never catch them."

"They would have slowed down considerably once they had reached the safety of Zambia. They will probably not reach their camp until tonight or given the state of the woman, possibly not even until tomorrow morning, and they will certainly rest for a few days before moving on again. We could catch them up in less than a day and a half – if we moved quickly."

Russell paused, not wanting to hear himself say the words, but they came anyway.

"Okay. Lets go!"

The two men headed off back towards the Zambesi river, coming to the dirt track that made up the river road. Russell noticed how expertly the man erased their spoor as they crossed. They stopped themselves just short of the river.

"We should wait here until night fall."

"Okay." agreed Russell, with an ever growing feeling that, even now, before they had crossed the river, his fate was completely out of his own control. He could only hope that this man whom he had entrusted with his life – for reasons he still could not fathom or understand – had the skill to keep them both out of trouble.

They slid down the trunks of two trees, facing one another. Both took deep drinks from their water bottles then Russell reached into his kidney pouch that amongst other useful items such as his ever faithful Swiss army penknife, a small torch and mending kit, contained emergency rations of two bars of chocolate and some biltong. It was a strip of this dried spiced meat that he offered to the man, who took it gratefully.

"So, what do I call you?"

"Within ZAPU I am known as Comrade Max."

Russell raised a quizzical eyebrow.

"We always take on a false name to protect our families from retribution by the whites."

The tone was matter of fact but the words drove a slither of consternation through Russell's body. What was he doing putting his life into the hands of this man who so obviously hated his colour?

Comrade Max noticed the hesitation. Having decided that this man, even clothed in a white skin, was his brother, he was anxious to make him feel at ease. He grinned, showing a perfect set of white teeth.

"But my family..." he nodded towards Russell's amulet, "...my family call me Sam. I am Sam, son of Nyati. And you? What name do you go by?"

Russell relaxed and returned the grin. "Russell. Russell Forester. So, tell me, how did you come to be in ZAPU ?"

Sam studied his boots for a time.

"By mistake, I think. I lived in a kraal the other side of Bulawayo in the Matopos Hills. My father was the village Headman. I was good at school and when I was fifteen, my father was approached by members of ZAPU. They said that they were looking for young men to train as teachers so that when the war of liberation was over, and the Country free, there would be schooling for all the children. They said they would send me to University, so my father let me go."

Sam fingered his amulet, a deep sadness filling his voice.

"It was the night before I left that my Father, not

knowing whether he would live to see my return, passed the amulet – and its sacred mission – to me." There was silence for a while before Sam resumed his story.

"I was taken across to Zambia, but once there, I was immediately put on a plane and taken to Russia."

"Russia!" So that explained the near-perfect English.

"Yes." Now there was an edge of bitterness to Sam's voice. "It was a great shock to realise that I was not to become a teacher of history but a teacher of terrorism. But that is what happened. Once there, there was no turning back." In Russia, he had written to his father, pleading to be allowed to return home. The letter had been taken by the Commandant who promised it would be delivered to his father, but of course it had been destroyed – just as his other letters had been destroyed – and he never heard from his father. It was when he knew that the letters had never been sent, would never be sent, that Sam had felt the strong sense of betrayal. He thus began to hate the freedom fighters and their paymasters almost as much as he loathed the arrogant whites, for in the name of freedom they had taken away the remnants of his childhood and lost him his family. Disillusioned, Sam had soon concluded that what the leaders were really doing was just building up their own political and military empires, power bases from which the ordinary African would gain nothing. He was positive that there had to be a better way of returning the land to its rightful people, he just didn't know what it was.

Sam had lapsed into deep thought but roused himself at Russell's question.

"What?"

"I said, you weren't happy there?"

"No." Sam gave a mocking smile. "But do not misunderstand me. In my own way, I am just as determined that our people should be free of the domination of you white settlers as they are. But the killing and coercion employed by my own people, this, too, is wrong. We should be free, really free. In the mind as well as the body." Sam gave a sigh and for a second time seemed far away.

"Anyway, I stayed in Russia for seven years."

"Seven years! What the hell were you doing for all that time?"

This question caused Sam's face to light up with a wicked grin.

"Learning ways to kill you, of course!" The glint of merriment died in his eyes and his face turned serious. "We learnt many things. We were trained in guns, tactics, explosives, indoctrination, anti-tracking, bush craft. I was transferred to the administrative side of the camp for a while but then there was a change in personnel and I was returned here. This was to be my first mission." He gave a short grunt. "Anyway, I think I am glad I failed."

Russell chuckled.

"So am I!"

The two men sat in silence for a while, chewing biltong, each caught up in his own thoughts. Sam took the opportunity to study the man opposite. He judged Russell to be six foot tall – and fit. He liked the direct look. A sign of a man who could be trusted. He had also seen the sorrow in Russell's face when he had been deep in thought prior to making his decision. Of course there was no way of telling what had caused such pain but Sam was convinced it had something to do with the war. Somehow Russell had suffered as he had suffered, and it was another strand in the invisible bond that tied them together. Sam broke the silence. It was his turn to be curious.

"And you, my friend, how did you come to wear the amulet?"

"Well, its a long story."

Sam, resting casually against his tree trunk, gave another dazzling grin and spread out his arms in an open gesture. "I don't think I have any pressing engagements for the next couple of hours."

Russell laughed. This was crazy. Here he was sitting with the enemy, sharing food and talking of childhoods and probably not far away, search parties were out looking for him, fearing him dead or taken prisoner. Once again the feeling that some greater force had taken over control of his life seeped through him, making crazy sense of his actions. It crossed his mind that his Superiors were unlikely to take the same viewpoint but that now seemed irrelevant. He took another bite of biltong, chewed for a while as he collected his thoughts and went back in time.

"I spent my childhood in Kenya, living with my parents in Nairobi......"

CHAPTER FIVE

He was back, back to being twelve years old. It was all so clear in his mind that he could have been talking about events that had occurred only the day before. In his mind's eye he could see the squat, green corrugated iron roofed bungalow that had been his home. Nestling in a garden full of bright tropical flowers alive with the movement of feeding iridescent sunbirds, the image seemed frozen in time. There, sitting on the long, cool verandah were his Mother and Father, drinking their sun-downers as he and his brother David played with Ben the Alsatian. Other long forgotten memories came flooding back. He could see the stately cape chestnut tree outside his bedroom window from where the doves cooed him awake every morning and could once again hear the gentle, rhythmic swishing sound of the garden boy's rake as he methodically swept the dead leaves from the lawn. He could also remember quite clearly the day that his friendship with Mukora had begun.

He had rushed home from school that Saturday lunch time, bolting down his food to be off on his bicycle, pedalling for all he was worth, down to Bradley's house. Russell was envious of his friend, for his house on the outskirts of Nairobi backed onto the wild bush and most weekends and holidays they went out together on collecting trips. Bradley was obsessed with snakes. Staying overnight at his house was a trial of friendship, the bedroom always being liberally littered with boxes and wicker baskets housing reptiles of varying size, colour and degrees of venom. On more than one occasion Russell had lain awake to the early hours of the morning listening to the constant rustling, tormenting himself with the thought that at any moment, the snakes would escape from their flimsy prisons.

On their outings, Brad would set off loaded down with his snake catching equipment, tongs – surreptitiously borrowed from his Mother's wash tub – forked sticks and nooses, assorted bags and boxes and a pair of his Father's old motorbike goggles in case he came across a spitting cobra! The protective gear was needed for Brad displayed a cavalier attitude to catching snakes that often horrified – and terrified – Russell. Spying an all but hidden snake in a bush, Brad would try to identify it but if he failed, would often decide that the best way forward was to put his arm into the bush, grab the snake and in one quick yank, pull it out of the bush. The unsuspecting snake would then fly into the air and with a loud thud, land on the ground. Most snakes, not unnaturally, became very ill-tempered at this treatment and Russell often wished his Father rode a bike so that he, too, could have protective goggles.

As for himself, Russell was an ardent collector of butterflies and birds eggs, and his equipment consisted of home made catching nets, jars and collecting bags he had pestered his Mother to make.

This particular day they set off towards a ravine they had discovered a few weeks before. It was a quiet, eerie place for it showed no sign of human presence even though some shambas were quite close and there was plenty of firewood readily accessible for collection.

To reach the ravine itself entailed the two boys walking down to the river through the old blue gum tree plantation, where the air was always heavy with the smell of eucalyptus. Elephant grasses, taller than the boys, over-hung the river bank and were full of movement and noise from the golden yellow weaver birds as they wove their dangling, elegant nests over the water and displayed to one another.

The crystal clear river had frogs and terrapins living

there and that afternoon Russell, as usual, spent several absorbed minutes examining the water and rocks to see if anything unusual could be found. However, deciding it would be better not to acquire too many specimens on the way up to the ravine, the boys continued their journey, crossing the water by jumping from one large, flat stepping stone to another. Both boys, more often than not, slipped on the algae covered rock and fell into the water, but in the heat of the African sun, it did not matter.

The shambas began on the other side of the river, the grassland now turned into a patchwork of maize, sweet potatoes, beans and chilli peppers. Russell and Brad, skirting the shambas, often heard the Kikuyu women laughing and chattering as they worked and hoed their lush gardens. Sometimes the women spotted the two boys and called out greetings, asking what important errand they were on.

After a short distance the shambas petered out and the cultivated land reverted back to thick bush. It was necessary for the boys to push their way through the rank vegetation in order to follow the course of the river. Negotiating a bend, the river unexpectedly opened up into a long pool some two hundred feet long by forty feet wide. To the left, a sheer cliff rose some sixty feet skyward whilst around its base, huge boulders that had crumbled from the rock face itself, littered the floor. These damp boulders were heavily blanketed in mosses, lichens and ferns whilst above them in the sunlight the rock face was abundantly covered in hanging epiphytes and creeping vines.

On the right bank of the pool there was a narrow flat strip of land, overgrown with giant clumps of bamboo, before another vertical wall of rock rose from the ground, forming a narrow ravine. At the far end of the pool, the gorge ended in a thirty foot solid wall of rock over which the river tumbled in a beautiful, glittering waterfall. It was possible to climb up the side of the fall and this revealed that the ravine continued up along the river before slowly giving way to hillside. To Russell it appeared like a miniature rain forest and he thrilled at the sight of it.

That day, after a short rest and drink of homemade orangeade, Brad went off to search amongst the nooks and crannies of the rocks whilst Russell pottered about collecting weaver bird nests that had fallen into the water, examining insects and attempting to capture butterflies with his net. Absorbed in their quests the boys parted company and Russell decided to clamber up the rocks to the top of the waterfall.

It was an exhausting climb, but having succeeded in reaching the top, he was rewarded with a magnificent view of the tranquil, sunlit gorge below. As he sat and rested, a duiker came out of the dappled shade of the high grass. Russell watched spellbound as the dainty antelope tested the air for danger before stepping elegantly to the water's edge. Even as it drank, the duiker's ears were in constant motion, alert for the slightest sound of danger.

A movement in the masses of convolvulus creeper growing on the rocks beside him caught Russell's eye and diverted his attention. With growing excitement, he drew his butterfly net to him and very, very slowly lifted it into the air. There on the convolvulus, flitting from one brilliant white flower to the next, was the most beautiful butterfly he had ever seen, its open wings sparkling in the sunlight like mother of pearl. It flitted teasingly close. Russell pounced. – and missed. The butterfly danced off and disappeared over the top of the ravine whilst the duiker, catching Russell's movement, darted back into the safety of the grass in a single lithe bound.

As Russell scoured the convolvulus for signs of the insect, he noticed, almost hidden behind the creeper, a small ledge running along the rock face that seemed to end in a fissure in the rock. Intrigued he was about to explore when he heard Brad, his voice just audible over the sound of the waterfall, calling from below. It was time to go.

All through the next week Russell's concentration on school work kept wavering in favour of wild fantasies built around the unusual butterfly and the mysterious ledge. As each dreary, miserable day passed, the excitement of discovery grew. Even when, as usual, he failed his Friday mathematics exam and had to report to Father O'Hara for a beating, the pain failed to dim his spirit of adventure.

He thought school would never end but finally it was Saturday afternoon again and he was free, but instead of being allowed to go to Brad's, his parents insisted he and David accompany them to a friend's house on the other side of the City. Infuriatingly, instead of the excitement of exploration, he had to sit and suffer an entire afternoon of tea and gossip.

Even the following day, he had to endure Sunday Mass and Sunday School before being able to swap his school uniform for a cooler open necked shirt and shorts. He cycled down to Brad's in a state of high excitement and it was just too much for him when he discovered that instead of waiting, Brad had gone off somewhere else with other friends. Frustrated, Russell decided to go it alone so he left his bike at Brad's and returned to the gorge by himself.

Arriving at the pool, he immediately climbed the waterfall and went straight to the ledge. Having made a bet with himself as he clambered up the rocks that the opening he had seen would probably turn out to be nothing more than a shadow, he was astonished to find himself looking into a deep fissure large enough to crawl through. It occurred to him that some dangerous animal might be lurking there, so it was with some trepidation that he forced himself to scramble through the gap.

He found himself in a small cave and as his eyes adjusted to the dim light, saw a rush sleeping mat, with some animal skins lying on top, a couple of pots and utensils neatly stacked against one wall and in the centre of the room, an unlit fire, surrounded by three smooth cooking stones. A small hole in the cave roof above the fire which let the smoke out also allowed a thin shaft of sunlight to filter through.

Russell felt a rush of disappointment. It would have made a perfect secret hideaway if it had been empty. What a discovery to boast about to Brad! But somebody already lived there. The full implication of what this meant gradually sank into Russell's consciousness and made him shiver with growing alarm. Who did live there? Where was he? Was he dangerous? Russell's nerve deserted him and he fled from the cave, out into the full warmth of the sunshine where his fear quickly evaporated.

Absorbed again with the beauty of the place and its wildlife, Russell forgot about the cave as he once more settled himself to wait and see if the Mother of Pearl butterfly would appear on the creeper. His patience was rewarded. The butterfly came and settled on the flowers in front of him. Once again Russell tried but failed to catch it.

His heart skipped several beats at the sound of someone laughing and turning towards the ledge, was startled to see an old African squatting there. With receding white woolly hair, eyes milky with age and leathery skin deeply wrinkled, he appeared incredibly ancient to the young Russell. His only clothing was a loin cloth and around his neck dangled a large pendant.

Recovering a little Russell got to his feet, speaking with all the authority he could muster.

"Are you laughing at me?"

The cackle continued.

"Ndiyo." Yes, the man answered in Swahili.

Russell was not able to think of a suitable reply so just stood, butterfly net in hand, staring down at the water whilst at the same time keeping a watchful eye on the old man.

"You'll never catch the butterfly with that." A thin arm pointed contemptuously at the net. "You need something longer but lighter – like the bamboo down there."

Russell went sullen. What had it got to do with the old man anyway?

The African chuckled again at the youngster's obvious discomfort. Then he spoke more seriously.

"You must be careful. This is a sacred place and the animals and insects are not hunted here. You must treat everything with great respect."

"What if I want to take the butterfly away with me? Who is going to stop me?"

"The spirits that watch over this place will know. It is not wise to upset them. They told me you came uninvited into my house."

Russell was more than a little disconcerted at being found out and began to fidget. He decided he didn't want to talk to the old man anymore. He wanted to go home. He edged his way to the point where he had to climb down.

"I've.., I've got to go now."

"Yes, but next time you come, be good enough to announce yourself before you enter my house. Kwaheri." Having said goodbye, the ancient man with surprising agility, rose and disappeared into the cave.

Chastened, Russell hurried home, telling no-one of his discovery, but the next Saturday he was back at the cave, this time making a lot of noise and calling out to the old man that he was there.

He offered a slice of fillet steak he had purloined from his mother's fridge, as an apology for his behaviour the week before and it was the start of a friendship that was to last for several months.

Whenever he could, Russell slipped off to visit the old African, Mukora, who filled Russell's head with stories of how Africa had been before the coming of the white man and all the changes that such a clash of cultures had brought. Mukora taught him about the bush and related the ancient stories concerning how the world began that had been passed down by word of mouth from one generation to the next.

"Do you know why there are black people and white people?"

"No."

"Well at the beginning of time everyone was black but then God started to paint, colouring people white. He finally came to two remote tribes. He sent a chameleon and a lizard to go and summon the tribes to him. The lizard went quickly but the chameleon was so slow that when the people eventually arrived, all the white paint had been used and all that was left was enough for the tribe to dip in their hands and feet. That is why black people have white palms and soles." Mukora raised his hands and feet for Russell to see then went into gales of laughter.

Then one Saturday Russell arrived to find Mukora lying on his bed. The sight of the old man, obviously ill, filled Russell with apprehension. He quickly fetched some fresh water and raising Mukora's head, persuaded him to take a drink.

Seeing the concern on Russell's face, Mukora tried to reassure him.

"Don't fret, boy. I'm just tired."

Russell gently lowered Mukora's head. The old man had closed his eyes and Russell thought he had fallen asleep so made to move away but a bony hand grabbed his arm with surprising force. Russell looked down and found Mukora looking intently at him.

"What is it, Mukora?"

"My time is running out. I am an old man, without a son or living relative and my own people are not interested in what I have to say. They are too busy learning the white man's ways and consider me a nuisance." Again, he squeezed Russell's arm so that Russell flinched with discomfort.

"*YOU* must listen to me!."

With great effort, the old man slowly took off the pendant that he always wore around his neck. He opened Russell's hand and placed the pendant in his palm, closing Russell's fingers tightly around it.

"This is a sacred amulet, blessed by the Spirits for those who wear it with honour. It has been passed from father to son down the generations, each wearer charged with keeping the vigil and telling the history."

"What vigil, Mukora? What history?"

"Once, a long, long time ago..."

"Before the white man came?" interjected Russell helpfully.

Mukora's face clouded over. "Be quiet! Don't keep interrupting and asking questions. Listen! This is not just another story. This is the truth and is very important. You must remember it correctly!"

Russell had never heard Mukora sound so solemn or look so grave. It made him feel uneasy and he wanted to go out into the bright, hot sunshine outside the cave, but Mukora still held his arm in a tight grip, so he had no option but to sit and listen.

"In the days of my ancestors, there was a mighty King who ruled over his people from a huge City far to the South of here. The people were rich and prosperous. They traded to the West and to the North. They had trade routes across the land and even further, to foreign lands, to the Arabs and to the East where the people have yellow skins. Caravans of goods moved across the land carrying gum arabic, spices, cloth, gold and ivory. Then a plague struck the kingdom. People died in their tens of thousands. They would go thin, thin like skeletons and die. The witch doctors of the Nation said that the kingdom had been cursed. The spirits were angry that they had been forgotten during the time of plenty and the people's wickedness must be punished. Nothing but death would appease them. The shamans prophesied the end of the nation – all would eventually die.

The King accepted the fate of his people. He ordered that the throne, the King's treasures and the great symbols of the City be removed to a safe place. He brought before him two hundred of his strongest, finest young warriors and charged them with keeping watch over the treasure. They vowed to pass on to their sons and to their sons, the history of the Kingdom until the day when it was safe to restore the treasures to their rightful place."

Russell was enthralled by the story. He had been to the flea pit cinema in Nairobi and seen Stewart Granger in 'King Solomon's Mines', living the adventure on the edge of his seat. His mind immediately pictured chests of gold, rubies and diamonds as big as a man's fist.

"The two hundred warriors carried out the King's order. Each received an amulet, blessed by the King's witch doctor, as a symbol of their authority and trust. They marched out of the City, far away to the North, away from the plague. They crossed a great river and travelled to a place that had been prepared. It was called the Valley of the Black Spear. The treasure was hidden in the rocks for safe keeping, then each warrior departed, leaving only a few to stand guard. All went in separate directions, away from their homeland to escape dying from the disease themselves for their duty was not done. It fell to these men to keep alive the history, to pass it down to their sons, and to their sons, until the day when the people would reclaim their Royal House."

Mukora had closed his eyes whilst he spoke, but now he looked at Russell, the milky eyes watching the boy's face intently.

"You have understood what I have said?"

"Yes, Mukora."

"You are sure?"

"Yes, Mukora, I'm sure."

"And you will remember it?"

"Yes."

"Good." He nodded as if satisfied. "Now, you must take the amulet and keep it safe until the day you find the right person to tell the history to, so that he may continue to keep faith with my forefathers and their sacred oath."

Russell aware of how important this odd request seemed to be to his friend, wanted only to reassure.

"I will, Mukora. I promise!"

The old man smiled up at the small, earnest face. The long speech had tired him.

"It is time for you to go and let me rest." He let go of Russell's arm and lifting his shaking hand, placed it on Russell's head. He spoke softly, changing from the Swahili they had been speaking to a language Russell had not heard before, but even though he could not understand the words, he was sure that Mukora was bestowing some kind of blessing.

"Go now."

"Goodbye, Mukora. I'll see you next week."

But the next week when Russell climbed up the rocks to the cave, there had been no sign of Mukora. Russell called out but his voice just faded, unanswered, into the roar of the waterfall. The cave was bare. No bedding, no utensils, no fire.

He went down to the shambas and asked the local women if they knew what had happened, but they only laughed, amused by the boy. Shaking their heads, they said they knew nothing of an old man living alone in a cave. No-one would live up there, they patiently explained to the agitated boy, it was a place of spirits. No African would go up there, for if they did, everyone knew they would come back mad.

Russell, reluctant to give up the search, returned to the cave the following week and the week after that, in the vain hope that he would find Mukora there. He smoothed the dust at the entrance of the cave and placed fine pieces of straw across the floor but when he returned, they were as he had left them with no sign of disturbance. It was as if Mukora had never existed.

Russell sat perched on the rocks, the stunning Mother of Pearl butterfly darting in front of him as it searched for nectar but for once Russell took no notice of it. Instead he took out the amulet from under his shirt. It was made out of bronze and had an intricate design of two cobras entwined, their necks hanging low with raised hoods. Beautifully detailed, the bodies were coiled around each other, their tails looping together to form a fastening for a leather thong to pass through.

Russell held the amulet in his two hands and with head bowed, let the burning tears of loss roll down his cheeks. Mukora had gone.

CHAPTER SIX

The two men sat in silence for a while after the conclusion of the story. Russell found it hard to bring his mind back to the present and talking of the past made the reality of his current circumstances seem even more bizarre. He re-examined the situation.

There was still time to go back. He could let Sam go, return to the camp and say he had lost the spoor. If he went a step further, he would be beyond the point of no return. As he listened to the nearby sounds of the river, another more practical worry entered Russell's head. The rainy season was upon them.

So far there had only been isolated thunder storms in the region, but that could change at any moment. Once the rains really started, the Zambesi would loose its lazy meandering ways and become a torrent of fast moving water with dangerous undercurrents that would make it virtually impossible for a man alone to cross. He could become stranded on the other side. Deep in his own thoughts, he jumped when Sam tapped him on the leg.

"The light is fading fast. If we are going, we should go now. We should aim to be across before the moon comes up." He paused. He knew now that Russell would not take him captive and there was genuine concern in his voice as he continued.

"There is still time for you to turn back my friend. No-one would know. There is no reason for you to risk your life over the South Africans. You are not to blame for their predicament."

But Russell's mind still held the memory of Sara. There had not been enough time for his feeling of guilt to subside. It was his fault she had died but now he had the chance, however remote, to save someone else. Whatever anyone else thought, whatever kind of trouble he would be in if he returned – it struck him how calmly his mind was thinking in terms of 'if' – he knew for his own peace of mind, he had to go.

He stood up, swinging his rifle on to his shoulder.

"Let's go."

They carefully made their way down to the river. Standing on the bank, Russell looked in amazement. He had become disorientated by the chase but now came to realise he knew exactly where he was. In fact on more than one occasion he had sat concealed in the undergrowth very near to this particular section of the river whilst on overnight observation patrol. Almost directly opposite from where they stood, an old settler's hunting lodge, built on a vantage point on the river bank, now served as a station outpost for the Zambian army. Russell had spent many a diverting hour with his binoculars trained on the Zambian soldiers as they drank and enjoyed themselves with women from the local shebeen.

"You do realise there is a Zambian army post right opposite us?"

"Yes. We cross just below them." Sam was busy taking off his boots. He paused, sensing Russell's hesitation, then tying his boot laces together, shrugged as if to say there was still time for Russell to back out.

"It is as safe as anywhere. This is where we cross."

Without waiting for Russell's reaction, Sam slung his boots around his neck and waded into the water. His new friend would either follow or stay behind. Either way, he was free. He held his rifle high above his head, careful to protect it from the water.

Russell continued to look doubtfully at the river bank as Sam's silhouette began to quickly merge into the surrounding darkness. Doubting time had run out. He had to act. Muttering a small prayer dug out from the recesses of his mind, Russell yanked his boots off and followed.

The water crept coldly up their bodies as the two men slowly and in silence, crossed the great river. It was sluggish at this point and they had several sand banks to negotiate. The main fear in both men was not that of being drowned but of being attacked by the many crocodiles that frequented the water. These large prehistoric creatures, looking harmless and clumsy enough as they rested up on the sand banks, could nevertheless slide stealthily into the water, submerge and, unseen until it was too late, clamp their massive jaws around a hapless body. Thus held, there was little chance of escaping a watery grave. Russell, having had the grim task of pulling decomposed bodies that had suffered such a fate from the Zambesi, could appreciate only too well the real danger lurking in the water. It was this thought more than any other that caused his heart to race and his eyes to nervously scan the water as they made their way, sand bank to sand bank, across to the other side.

Both men exhaled in relief as they reached the safety of the far bank. Pausing to get their bearings, Russell looked warily to his left towards the Army post. There were lights showing in the windows and the faint muffled sounds of several voices could be heard. Parked outside and illuminated clearly by the house lights, Russell registered a Landrover painted in a gaudy camouflage of green with orange dots.

Sam tapped him on the shoulder and gestured that they should climb the bank. Russell nodded and Sam began to haul himself up the steep bank, Russell following as closely behind as he could. Deep in concentration the two men tried to gauge where the safest footholds were.

Having made good progress, Sam abruptly stopped, almost causing Russell to yell out in surprise as he collided with Sam's legs. From the direction of the Army Post, a stronger shaft of light shone out into the darkness and the voices became louder. Someone had opened the door of the lodge.

Sam and Russell flattened themselves to the ground, tucking their rifles in beside their bodies and, resisting the urge to look up, kept their heads down. But to their growing alarm, they heard a group of rowdy soldiers bid a noisy farewell to their comrades and begin to stumble along in the dark towards the spot where they lay. The soldiers had almost walked right past when one staggered to a stop and turned himself towards the bank.

Trying to subdue their breathing and will themselves to merge even further into the cover of the bank, Sam and Russell could only pray that they would not be detected. The soldier jokily call out to the others who all laughed and carried on walking.

Immediately Russell felt something warm and wet fall down the back of his shirt. His mind registered what it was.

'The drunken bastard's peeing on me!' Russell struggled against the almost overwhelming desire to move or call out as the pungent liquid continued to rain down on him. He tightened his grip around the stock of his rifle, conscious of Sam's eyes burning into him, willing him to keep still at all costs. Even so, it was all he could do to suffer the indignity in silence.

At last the man finished urinating and unaware of just how close to sudden death he had come, noisily hurried off to catch up with his comrades.

Waiting to make sure the soldiers were well out of sight, Sam moved up to the top of the bank and checked the post. All now seemed quiet. He hoarsely whispered down to Russell.

"Go straight across and wait for me about a hundred yards inland."

Russell did as he was bid. He was now completely in the hands of Sam. He had to trust him. As he scrambled to the top of the bank, he could make out the wide dirt track but it was now so dark, he could not see the scrub on the other side.

He crossed the track in his bare feet, stepping sideways so that it might look like someone walking forward. The road was obviously well used so his and Sam's tracks would become one of many. Better still, if lady luck was on their side, a light shower might obliterate all traces for them. Russell stepped carefully over the middle of the track and from the safety of the bush on the other side, put his boots on as he waited for Sam to join him. Reaching the scrub himself, Sam snapped off a branch and for several hundred yards, walked back to back with Russell, expertly sweeping their tracks from the ground.

By now the rising moon emitted enough light for them to zig zag their way into the interior, keeping well clear of any human habitation. The bush seemed to be very similar to that on the Rhodesian side of the river and it was easy for Russell to pretend to himself that he was still in familiar territory.

For four hours they continued to walk in a North-Easterly direction then, exhausted, they crawled into a dense area of thorn scrub, the vicious thorns tearing at their clothing as they pushed themselves through. Protected by the thorns, the ground underneath was a mass of small animal trails leading to a small clearing in the centre and it was here that they fell gratefully to the ground, sharing the last of Russell's biltong before curling up to sleep.

The laughing whoop of an hyena in the distance took Russell's mind back to just over twenty four hours before when he had lain in the Rhodesian bush listening to another hyena, wondering what daylight would bring. Not even in his wildest fantasy would he have imagined it would have ended with him being in Zambia, next to the terrorist he had been chasing, both having had the opportunity to kill the other. But at last the day's events finally caught up with him, his mind became fuddled and he drifted into sleep.

When he awoke, the sun was rising rapidly, shedding dappled light through the thorn scrub. Russell's brain, still foggy from sleep, took a moment to register where he was. He turned his head to where he thought Sam would be but with a jolt realised he was alone. Sam had gone! Frantic, he reached out with his arm and touched the butt of his rifle – it was still by his side! Momentarily relieved, he sat up, stretched out his legs and rubbed his face vigorously. He was surprised to feel the strong stubble on his cheeks and chin. It had now been two days since he had shaved. He tried a pep talk to himself. He was not to panic. He was alone in the middle of enemy territory without the faintest idea of where he was, but there was no need to panic.

He shook his head and drawing his legs up, rested his arms on his knees. His instructor's words, spoken in jest during one of the early lessons in Training Depot, concerning what to do if you got caught by the enemy came flooding back to haunt him.

"If you inadvertently cross a very wide river and get caught, die like a man – cry, pray, beg, scream, plead....." It had caused a great deal of mirth in the classroom, but now it did not seem so funny and he felt a sick churning feeling in the pit of his stomach. He reached for his water bottle. It had gone. Trying to quell his rising anxiety, he checked his ammunition and his kidney pouch. The last bar of chocolate was still there. He heard a twig snap. Instantly he was fully alert and in one smooth action grabbed his rifle and eased the safety catch off. A low whistle, more movement in the bush, then a whisper.

"It is Sam."

Unimaginable relief flooded through Russell as

Sam's – and only Sam's – head appeared through the thicket.

"Shit man! You had me going there for a moment!"

"Sorry." apologised Sam, a broad grin spreading across his face. "Here."

He handed Russell his two water bottles. They were full. Russell gratefully took a swig out of one, swished the refreshing cool water around his mouth, spat the residue out then vigorously rubbed his teeth with two fingers, trying to clean off the accumulated layer of dust and grime stubbornly clinging to them. He then poured some water into the cup of his hand and splashed it over his face.

"Thanks..... What have you got there? Breakfast?"

"No." Sam had laid down some bunches of dark purple-black berries and was now busily de-stemming them.

"Right, hold out your hands."

Russell, mystified, did so. Sam placed the berries in his palms.

"Now, crush them and wash your face and hands in the juice."

Russell hesitated. "What?"

"Do not forget. You are in Zambia now. Zambia as in Black Man. There are no whites left around here. Close up, you are not going to fool anyone, but with your face and hands blackened, if you are seen from a distance, you will probably get away with it. This is a military training zone – men in fatigues wandering about are a common sight and do not raise any suspicions. Oh, and you had better get rid of those."

He was pointing at the BSAP epaulets on Russell's shoulders.

Russell squashed the berries in his hands then quickly covered his face, neck and hands in the black acerbic liquid. He could feel his skin pull tight as it began to dry. He took off the epaulets from his shirt, held them in his hand for a moment – it was better not to think too long about them – and buttoned them into his top pocket. He then unfolded the neck flap on his cap and rolled down the sleeves of his uniform, for once thankful that battle fatigues looked very similar no matter who wore them. Otherwise he had no doubt Sam would have stripped him down to his underpants and covered his entire body with the foul dye. As it was, Sam was having trouble keeping a straight face as he surveyed the results of Russell's labour.

"Sorry, but I think perhaps it is just as well you can not see yourself in a mirror!" He sobered, his face turning grave. "If we are to make up ground on the gang, we will need to move fast."

"Right. I guess I'm as ready as I'll ever be." Russell rummaged in his kidney pouch, bringing out the bar of chocolate. He broke it in half and handed one piece to Sam. "Here, its not much but I'm afraid its all thats left."

They ate as they crawled back out of the tangled thicket.

"We will have to back track a few hundred yards to pick up the the trail again." Sam led the way and quickly came to a well worn path. "This is it. This is the track we follow."

The flat open bush made it possible for Sam to set a fast pace and steady progress was made through the day. Twice they saw groups of men walking in the far distance and quickly dropped down into cover until all was clear. They saw no other humans and only a small herd of impala shared the path with them. Russell was not sure whether the lack of game was because the herds had dispersed ahead of the coming rains or that the army and terrorists had shot them out for food. Once Russell looked behind him and could still see, as a thin pale purple line on the horizon, the Rhodesian escarpment. It seemed to belong to another time and another life.

It was late into the afternoon, the sun having already lost the worst of its fierce heat when a bestial scream stopped them in their stride. Russell dropped into cover on the left, Sam to the right. Both brought their rifles up, slipping the safety catches off in readiness. Silence.

For five tense minutes they waited.

"What do you think? A baboon or monkey being taken?" The edge on Russell's cracked whisper betrayed the anxiety he felt.

"Yes. That must have been it." Sam's reply was just as strained.

"But listen, Russell, we are getting near the area where the camp is suppose to be. We had better go more carefully from now on."

"Right. Understood."

They moved off, alert, eyes searching the bush ahead. Russell's heart began to regulate itself back to a steady rhythm but a second scream breaking the harsh silence around them, caused his pulse to race and the painful thumping in his chest to begin again. This time they could not pretend it was anything other than a human being crying out in unendurable pain. They both knew what the scream meant.

Without speaking, they left the path, moving into the bush. They slowly edged towards the source of the scream and as the land rose gently, they dropped down into the grass cautiously crawling forward on their elbows until they found themselves at the top of a ridge overlooking a small clearing that had been turned into a makeshift camp site.

Russell counted eight sleeping mats but could only see six men. Four were sitting, laughing and drinking beer around a large fire that had pieces of skewered antelope roasting over the flames. They were relaxed and had no sentries, obviously believing themselves on safe ground and beyond the reach of their enemies.

But it was the remaining two that gripped Russell's attention. They were standing, casually smoking and drinking, in front of a tree on which, strung up by his arms, was a man. He was white but his naked body was covered in dried black blood with fresh scarlet rivulets running down his chest. Even though his head was bowed, Russell could see he had had his eyes gouged out. Across his chest were deep knife wounds and his groin was covered in blood. Russell wanted to retch. As he watched, mesmerised by the horror, one of the men took his bayonet and casually pierced the man in the groin, giving rise to another ear-piercing scream that shuddered all the way through Russell's body.

He forced his eyes away and gave the camp another sweep. There! Almost hidden by the large tree he was bound to and missed in the first scan of the camp, a young African boy sat looking stone-faced towards the activities at the nearby tree to his left. Russell stared harder and was positive he could make out a white arm showing from around the trunk too. It had to be the woman.

Russell tugged on Sam's arm and they crawled back to a safer distance from the ridge top. Both men were visibly disturbed.

Russell tried to whisper but his throat was too constricted. He painfully swallowed and tried again. This time words came out, but his voice held a quiver of revulsion he could not control.

"Did you see the woman and boy tied to the tree?"

"Yes." Sam's voice was no steadier than Russell's. He felt angry and ashamed. Not because it was a black man causing such suffering for he knew the whites could be just as senselessly vindictive, but because any member of the human race could behave with such barbaric and unnecessary cruelty.

"The boy looked all right – but in shock." Russell added.

Sam, not trusting his voice, nodded.

Another sickening scream galvanised Russell.

"We're going to have to mount an immediate rescue."

"What! Are you crazy? There are six, maybe eight of them and only one of you. You don't stand a chance."

"Two of us." Russell stubbornly corrected.

Sam recoiled, his undertone defiant.

"Oh, no! I said I would bring you to the camp and take you back to the Zambesi. There was nothing in our deal that said I had to get my balls blown off in the middle as well!"

"All right, I can't make you do anything. You'd better stay here and wait for me to get back." The two men glared at each other for several long seconds before Russell sullenly spoke again. "You can at least give me two of your grenades."

Without comment, Sam pulled the grenades from his webbing and handed them to Russell, who examined them.

"Russian?"

Sam nodded.

"Well, I hope they're more reliable than their bloody guns!" Russell hooked the grenades onto his own webbing and began to crawl back towards the ridge.

Sam muttered an obscenity to himself as he watched Russell, knowing his denial of help was just a moment's aberration caused by the hopelessness of the situation. Of course in the back of his mind he had always known it would end in a fight – the gang were hardly going to hand the hostages over on request – and he could not stand by and let Russell attempt the rescue alone. It was those damn amulets again!

Accepting his fate, he stirred himself to go after

Russell, catching him and pulling him back from the ridge by the straps on his webbing.

"Wait a minute! What are you going to do?" Sam hissed.

"What's it got to do with you?" Russell hissed back. "When you hear this lot go off and I don't re-appear, run like hell!" He went to move off but once again was pulled back by his webbing. Sam was more insistent.

"What are you going to do!"

Russell sighed, shrugging his shoulders. "Lob the grenades and hope for the best."

"Good at cricket then were you?"

Even though it was muttered under Sam's breath, Russell heard the sardonic remark and showed his irritation by starting back up the ridge without further comment. He didn't need to be told that his plan was rather weak but discussing it would not improve matters. There was little else he could do. He had surprise on his side and with luck that would give him the advantage he needed. His progress was halted by a movement beside him and another harsh whisper in his ear.

"It was my way of asking whether you were any good at throwing grenades."

Another shrug from Russell before he answered through clenched teeth. "So-so. Happy now?"

"No, but you had better give me the grenades anyway." Sam saw the exasperated look on Russell's face. "Trust me, I am good."

Russell paused. Having experienced the stone throwing accuracy of the Africans during the Pierce Commission riots, he conceded the point to Sam and handed back the grenades. Sam slid back down the bank, once more leaving Russell no option but to do the same. Russell expanded his plan.

"What I was thinking of doing was lobbing the first grenade at the four by the fire, aiming it between them and the stores behind in the hope that it explodes any spare ammunition as well. The second grenade is for the two by the tree. If its pitched just short, it should at least knock them off their feet and hopefully the tree will shelter the woman and boy from the worst of the blast. Then, before the bastards can get their wits about them, I'll have my rifle ready to pick them off."

Sam's eyes widened and his jaw silently dropped open as he listened to Russell. He recovered enough to ask.

"Just how many American movies have you been watching lately?"

"Ha, ha! Very funny. It might not be the most complete plan ever devised but have you got a better idea?"

Sam puckered his brow, bit his upper lip, then sucked in his lower lip. Finally.

"No."

"Right. So are you going to lob the grenades?" Sam nodded. "Good. Give me time to move down and get as near to the camp as I dare, then let rip."

Russell felt the restraining hand on his shoulder as he went to move. Having steeled himself for action, he turned in fury.

"What now!"

"What about the other two?"

"What other two?"

"Unless I can not count there are eight beds and only six men."

"Maybe they've gone off hunting or gone to town or something. How the hell should I know?"

"Do you think we should wait and find out?"

Another scream answered their question. The two men edged their way to the top of the ridge and this time Russell flattened himself on the ground and wriggled inch by inch down the slope towards the camp.

Sam watched Russell snake down. He was good and no-one appeared to become alert to the imminent danger.

"Easy, Russell, easy. Nice and easy." He muttered to himself as one of the camp fire sitters got up and moved to the back where the supplies were stacked. Russell froze. The man collected an armful of bottles and sauntered over to the two men by the tree. Here, as the other two helped themselves to the offered beer, he stood jeering at the blood stained body of the man hanging on the tree. Russell could feel the bile rising in his throat. 'Just one more minute, you bastards, then I'll give you something to really laugh about!'

The three by the fire impatiently called out and the bottle carrier staggered back to them. Russell waited until the camp had settled down again before continuing his crawl. He reached the edge of the clearing and then under cover of a bout of laughter slipped over the safety catch on his rifle. No-one saw or heard him.

He looked back and raised a thumb to Sam, who signalled back. Russell brought the sight to his eye and with his finger on the trigger, waited. 'Right you buggers, let's see you get out of this one.'

Sam steadied himself against a tree and forced his mind to blank out everything other than the matter in hand. He took one deep, deep breath, held it for several seconds then exhaled slowly. Now totally focussed, he eased out the pin of the first grenade and turning to face the camp, lobbed it with as much force as he could muster towards the camp fire sitters. The moment it left his hand, he smoothly took another grenade from his webbing, pulled the pin and threw it towards its intended target. It was flying through the air as the first one landed behind the camp fire.

The men around the fire stopped their drinking to stare stupidly at the object that had just arched over their heads to land with a gentle thud behind them but their alcohol befuddled brains could not react quickly enough. Within seconds, a massive explosion rocked the camp, throwing bodies into the air, as instantaneously a further explosion erupted from the supplies. The second grenade landed too short, but the two men by the tree had already instinctively thrown themselves onto the ground, covering their heads with their hands in a useless attempt at protection, as the earth errupted around them.

Russell waited for the smoke to start to clear. One man was staggering around where only moments before the camp fire had offered comfort. Russell pumped several shots into him and the man fell. The two by the tree raised their heads, a look of uncomprehending fear on their faces. Russell held back until they had pulled themselves to their knees then emptied his magazine into them. Both men collapsed back to the ground in a heap and did not move again.

By the time Sam had joined Russell, he had already reloaded his FN and together they rushed into the camp. One man had died from his injuries but the remaining two were still alive, dazed and moaning loudly as they lay bleeding and shattered in the dust. Russell stood over them and fired at point blank range. Satisfied, he moved swiftly over to where the woman and boy sat, still staring in blank horror towards the tortured man as if unable to register the events that had just taken place. Human remains and other debris lay scattered about them but they were unharmed. The shrapnel peppered tree they were tied to had indeed sheltered them from the main force of the blasts.

Russell and Sam released the bonds but at first neither moved. At the insistent command of Sam, the boy, like a robot, stood up but the woman remained motionless on the ground. Russell bent down, grabbed her arms and pulled her up. She immediately crumpled back down to the ground. Her legs were completely useless. Without trying again, Russell irreverently hoisted her onto his shoulder. They pushed the boy ahead of them towards the man on the tree. He was still breathing but was now unconscious. Weakened by the loss of blood and wounded beyond help by the torture that had been inflicted on him over the hours, he had also been mutilated by the flying shrapnel.

"Poor sod." Russell stood momentarily mesmerised by the awful spectre in front of him. Sam roughly shoved him.

"Take the woman and boy and head out in that direction." Sam nodded towards the bush behind the camp. "We had better not go directly back the way we came. If the others are around, they will certainly have heard the commotion. Hurry!"

Russell looked in despair at the man he was unable to help, then looked at Sam. They had to do something.

"Go! Go! I will follow."

Russell nodded, understanding. He moved off at half a run, the adrenalin keeping him going. He called the boy to follow and thanked an unknown god that the boy obeyed.

In all, the raid had taken less than five minutes.

CHAPTER SEVEN

Russell carried the woman as far as he could until the stitch in his side forced him to stop. With eyes stinging from the effects of the explosion and heart thumping wildly from exertion, he felt as if his lungs were about to burst. Breathing heavily in short, painful gasps, he carefully lowered the woman down onto her feet, resting her against a tree. Her eyes were still blank and immediately he started to pull away from her, she began to slide back towards the ground. He caught her by her two arms and roughly shook her, speaking in an urgent, harsh undertone.

"Come on, lady. Come on! I need you on your feet!"

The shaking seemed to penetrate the woman's mind. She looked at Russell, her eyes focusing on him for the first time and he could feel some resistance return to her body.

He spoke slowly, patiently.

"I'm Patrol Officer Forester from the Rhodesian BSA Police. Do you understand?"

She managed a vague nod.

"I've come to take you home."

Continuing to stare at Russell in mute astonishment, the woman merely nodded her head again to acknowledge that she had heard what Russell had said.

"Can you walk?"

He relaxed his grip on her. She wobbled for a few seconds but, by putting a hand against the tree trunk, managed to steady herself and remain standing.

Lisa felt her mind start to break out of the numb, dense fog it had withdrawn into for the past few days. She tried to speak, but no sound came out. Raising a shaking hand to her throat, she gingerly touched the deep cut encircling her neck. Russell saw the wince of pain cut across her face as her hand touched the deep wound.

"Here, try some of this."

Russell opened his water flask and helped her to take a drink. He then turned to the boy who had hung back a little and offered him the flask. The boy took it and drank without a word.

"Okay. We've got to move. Do you think you'll be able to walk?"

Lisa wetted her dry, cracked lips with her tongue and tried to speak again. A sound, a sort of rasping whisper, unrecognisable to her as her own voice, came from her mouth.

"Yes. I think so. I've got pins and needles in my legs now and the feeling is coming back."

"Are you Lisa Barnard?"

She nodded. It hurt too much to talk if a nod would suffice.

Russell turned his attention to the boy.

"And you?"

There was no response from the boy other than to hand back the water bottle. Russell drank, trying to rid himself of the acrid taste of cordite in his throat but nothing could take away the distinctive stench of mutilated human corpses that lingered in his nostrils. Speaking more gently, he tried again with the boy.

"We have to call you something."

Lisa replied for him.

"His name is Seki."

There was a rustling in the vegetation behind them. Russell did not bother to react. If it wasn't Sam, there was little he could do, he was in no position to fight. He saw the flash of extreme terror go across the woman's face as she saw a large African come out of the bush, walking backwards towards them.

"It's all right. This is Sam. He's .... he's our guide."

"Where's Bob?"

The two men exchanged glances. Sam carefully arranged the branch he had used to sweep away their tracks into a bush to disguise the fact that it had been broken off another whilst Russell quietly replied.

"I'm sorry, he's dead."

Lisa let out a small whimper of distress and swayed on her feet so that Russell reached out to grab her arms again for fear that she would fall.

"Come on Lisa." His voice was steady, authoritative. "There's nothing we can do for Bob now. We've got to get you and the boy out of here." He looked to Sam.

"There is probably about an hour's daylight left. I think Russell, we should keep going away from the camp until dark, rest and then in the morning make a big loop around the area, back to the crossing. It may take a little longer, but I think it will be a safer route for you."

"I agree. By the way, this is Lisa Barnard and Seki."

Sam nodded curtly to Lisa. "Can you walk?"

"Yes."

"Okay, we must try and get as much distance as possible between us and the camp. Hopefully if anyone comes looking, they will expect us to be heading straight back towards the river." He paused, looking at Lisa, weighing up whether she was able to answer his question. He tried.

"There seems to be two men missing from the camp."

She nodded then seeing that more was needed, summoned the energy to explain.

"Yes, the leader and one of his men. They left camp this morning. I don't know for sure, but the way everyone kept looking in my direction as they argued, I have a feeling it had something to do with me."

"Yes, probably. It is likely that they have gone to

one of the main Training Camps in order to notify their Headquarters that they have a white hostage available." He saw Lisa shudder and added, hoping to reassure, "In which case I think it is highly unlikely they would return to the camp the same day."

It was also a comforting thought to Sam and Russell. To believe that the missing two gang members might not be in the immediate vicinity would, if they were lucky, give them anything up to twenty four hours head start before the raid was discovered. It certainly meant they had a better chance of getting through the night.

Sam became restless.

"All the same, Russell, I think we have wasted enough time here. We ought to make a move. Lets go." He turned his attention to the boy who was still standing quietly to one side.

"Seki, follow me."

They set off, moving north away from the camp, Russell at the rear, half pushing, half carrying Lisa forward. He was pleased to see that she had at least been sensible enough not to have worn high heel shoes. It never ceased to amaze him how many women, visiting out in the remote areas, dressed as if they were in fact going shopping in down-town Salisbury. Most seemed totally unaware of the rigours of the bush or be in any way prepared in case of a breakdown or trouble.

The weary group battled on until the fast fading light began to make their passage difficult. They found cover in a glade of ancient, grotesquely swollen baobab trees and settled down for the night.

Sam gratefully dropped a large canvas bag to the floor.

"I didn't notice you carrying that before."

"No." He grinned at Russell. Squatting on his heels, he delved into the bag and brought out some cooked meat and cakes of cold sadsza. "Seemed a shame to leave this behind in the camp with no-one to eat it."

Russell grinned back. He was famished. The boy too seemed happy to eat but Lisa refused her offered share.

"Come on, you've got to eat something." coaxed Russell. He leaned across, making her take a small piece of meat in one hand and sadsza cake in the other. "For maize porridge, it tastes surprisingly good." he encouraged.

As he offered the food, Russell looked closely at Lisa for the first time. She was wearing denim jeans and a sleeveless open necked blouse, originally white but now dirty and blood stained with numerous small rips in it where the thorn bushes had caught it. Her arms were scratched and badly burnt from exposure to the sun. He reckoned she was about five foot six, naturally slim and in her mid twenties. Even through the smudged and strained pallor, he saw an attractive blond with long legs that in more normal circumstances would certainly have raised his interest.

He wanted to ask her about what had happened to them since the mine blast, but knew his curiosity would have to wait. It was neither the time nor the place. Uncertain as to whether they were near any enemy positions, unnecessary talk or noise would be foolish but in any event, she looked too fragile to question.

Lisa nibbled at her piece of meat. She had no appetite, no energy to chew, her neck stung constantly and her throat hurt. She dared not take her safari boots off to look, but her feet felt as if they were raw and swimming in liquid. A mixture, she assumed, of blood and puss from burst blisters. She wanted to block out the last few days from her mind but every time she closed her eyes, she saw Bob Martin and could hear his horrendous screams of unimaginable pain as his eyes were put out, one and then the other. She began to quietly sob.

Russell pulled her to him and closed his arms around her. She was shaking and her tears soaked his shirt. She felt as cold as marble to the touch and he wanted to rub his hands over her bare arms to try and draw some warmth back to them but afraid of causing more pain to the scratched and blistered limbs, settled for just rocking her gently as gradually the sobbing subsided and she fell into an exhausted sleep. He gently moved her onto the ground then curled up next to her so that his body offered some protection against the chill of the night air.

He was awakened by the sound of thunder. His outstretched right arm had lost all feeling from the weight of Lisa's head on it. As he lay in the complete darkness, listening to the low distant rumblings, he prayed that it would not be the beginning of the rains. 'Please, God,' he silently, fervently, beseeched, 'let it be just another light rain storm in the hills.'

In time the thunder lessened then gradually ceased altogether, leaving the sounds of the night once more to the tree frogs and crickets. Funny, he thought, how such small insignificant creatures could make such a loud noise. At night they were as much the sound of Africa as the high pitched humming of the cicadas were by day.

His mind floated between sleep and full awareness. Chirundu came to the fore front of his mind and he idly thought about the place and its people. It was a small, one-horse town, especially now since, in a useless attempt to stop the terrorists incursions, Smith had closed the border, making the suspension bridge across the Zambesi a point of confrontation between the Zambian Army and the Rhodesian Police. The town itself consisted of nothing more than the Police and Immigration Messes standing in isolation at the top of the hill with, half way down, the South African camp. In the valley below lay a small African township with the police station, a customs and immigration border post, a telephone exchange and the motel, now empty and deserted by visitors.

'Poor old Bernie', thought Russell with a hitherto unknown sympathy for the plight of the owner, an ex-white hunter, who had ploughed his life's savings into the venture only to see the border closed shortly after the motel opened. Now the only life there was the chattering baboons and vervet monkeys which, in the absence of human activity, had made their roost in the trees above the chalets. Russell felt a longing to be back, sitting in the Mess bar, called with Rhodesian originality 'the water hole', supping ice cold beers and talking in endless circles on the subject of women, the bush and guns. It seemed so far away that he had difficulty in believing he might be back there tomorrow night or at the most, the day after. 'If our luck holds!' was his final thought as he drifted back into sleep.

The boy, Seki, was looking solemnly at him as he opened his eyes. He extracted his arm from under Lisa's head then waved it in an extravagant circular motion to try and bring some feeling back.

"Morning, Seki." He smiled at the boy who remained solemn and silent. Russell looked about him. "Where's Sam gone?"

The boy merely pointed beyond the baobabs towards the bush.

As Russell wondered whether it was worth trying the question again, Sam came into view, grinning with good humour.

"If you are interested, there is a small group of rocks just behind us that makes a good place to go and relieve yourself."

"Thanks." Russell looked down at the still sleeping Lisa. It seemed a pity to wake her, she probably needed at least twenty four hours sleep to recover from her ordeal, but they did not have that much time. He gently shook her shoulder. She woke with a start and would have screamed aloud had Russell not quickly put his hand over her mouth to stifle the sound.

"It's all right. You're safe with us. Remember?"

Lisa shivered as her mind cleared and nodded that she was all right.

Russell let his hand fall. "Sam says there's a good place to go and brush up, just behind the rocks there."

Lisa nodded and rose. She felt incredibly stiff and found it difficult to stand up straight. As she made to move forward, pain shot up her legs from her feet causing her to let out an involuntary cry.

Russell was immediately concerned.

"Are you okay?"

"Yes. Yes, I'm fine. Just stiff and sore." Her voice had returned to near normal. It was surprisingly deep, rich, almost sultry with a light South African lilt to it. 'Sexy' registered in Russell's brain.

Lisa hesitated. "I know I'm being silly but I'm afraid to go alone. Will you come with me? Please!"

The combination of the voice and the look she gave him, would have had Russell fighting a lion in single combat for her. He nodded his agreement and held out his hand to help her.

They crossed to the rocks. Russell turned his back in what he hoped would be taken as a gentlemanly act and Lisa was grateful for his consideration. With a blinding flash of anger she bitterly remembered the humiliating loss of dignity she had had to suffer in front of her tormenting captors. She wondered whether she would ever rid herself of the sense of degradation. Her thoughts were cut short by Russell calling her.

She came up to him, a light blush on her cheeks.

"Thank you." She made a start back to the makeshift camp, hobbling painfully as she went.

"Are you sure you're all right? We've got a lot of walking to do today."

She half turned round to face Russell. Determination, the kind that had probably stood her forefathers in good stead on the great trek North, was stamped across her features.

"If it means getting out of this place, I'll crawl on hands and knees if needs be!" Her face suddenly relaxed and a broad smile appeared as she continued to study Russell.

"I'm sorry, but I just have to ask. What is that on your face?"

"What?" Russell, now at Lisa's side, raised his hand to his cheek which was burning with embarrassment. He had completely forgotten about the berry stain. "Is that still there?"

"Yes, I'm afraid so!" Lisa licked her finger and rubbed his forehead. "And, I hate to say this, but I don't think its going to come off!"

They both laughed easily, Russell pleased that he had been the cause of the first smile to cross her face since the rescue operation.

"Okay. Come on, lets get some breakfast. How does cold antelope and sadsza grab you?"

Lisa grimaced. "Wonderful."

Their meagre breakfast finished, the four set off again through the vastness of the tall grassy open woodland that was punctuated with baobab trees whose stubby branches forever made the trees look as if they had been planted upside down. The boy and woman, placed in the middle, stumbled along, heads down, struggling to keep up with the pace set by Sam.

As the heat of the day bore down, it seemed to Lisa that they were walking inside a fiery furnace. The very air that she breathed seemed hot and debilitating. She closed her mind to everything other than placing one pitiful foot in front of the other and staying upright. She would make it, she told herself over and over. She would make it!

Sam at the head and Russell at the rear, walked with eyes and minds alert for any sign of movement that could spell danger. Once again Russell registered how little game there appeared to be in comparison to the Rhodesian side of the Zambesi valley. Every hour they stopped briefly to drink water and once, for a longer spell, to eat a few mouthfuls of meat. Lisa rested against a tree, refusing to sit down.

"If I do," she explained simply, "I'll never get back up again."

In weary silence they trudged on untill daylight once more began to desert them. Russell was struggling against bouts of dizziness. It was his seventh straight day of trekking and he was utterly exhausted. He urged himself to stay alert and to keep going and wished he had Sam's stamina.

Sam called to him.

"We can either rest up for the night, or attempt to carry on in the dark."

"How far do you reckon we are from the river?"

Sam thought, his brow furrowed in concentration.

"Not far in a direct line but the route we are taking will bring us out about a mile further up from the crossing point. I reckon we have another three miles to go. In daylight, with Lisa, that would be maybe two hour's walk, a little less if all went well. But at night...three hours at best, more likely four." He looked up at the rapidly darkening sky. "But if it remains a clear night, the moon should give us enough light."

"Would it leave us enough time to cross? I don't fancy being a hundred yards from the Army Post in broad daylight."

"If we rest now for say three hours and set off again about nine, that should give us ample time."

Russell felt renewed energy within him as he contemplated the nearness to the end of his journey. He looked towards Lisa, admiring her pluckiness in walking without complaint all day. But he had to be careful not to push her too far.

"Well, Lisa, its up to you. How do you feel? Walking is difficult enough for you now, but in the dark its going to be twice as bad."

The temptation of being back in Rhodesia by daylight tormented Lisa as much as it did Russell. It was so, so close.

She nodded, attempting to sound more positive that she felt. "I'm all for going. I can't believe my feet can get any worse."

"Seki?"

The boy, who had not spoken all day, nodded his agreement. Physically, at least, he seemed to be coping well with the walk.

"Agreed then, we give it a go?"

"Agreed."

"Agreed."

They dropped to the ground and Sam handed each a ration of cold meat to chew. No-one spoke, preferring to attempt a few hours sleep. Russell strained his ears to hear the tell-tale signs of thunder which would mean a cloudy sky and the end of their chances of going. But he heard nothing and to his immense relief, watched the moon come up in a clear sky. He uncrossed his legs, pulling his knees to his body, then folding his arms across his knees, rested his head. 'Five minutes' he said to himself as he closed his stinging eyes. 'Just five minutes rest.' He felt himself falling and his head jerked up, jolting him awake. Momentarily confused with sleep, he rubbed his eyes and reorientated himself.

Sheltering his watch with his hand, he was amazed to see the glowing green hands give the time as five to nine. He had been asleep for over two hours. He rose from the ground, his entire body aching, his mind sluggish from the effect of too little sleep. He shook himself awake and studied the darkness. It was just possible to see a little ahead, enough he thought, to gauge where they were going. They just had to hope that after two days of gameless trekking, tonight would not be the time they stumbled across a pride of lions or, worse still, walk into the middle of a herd of elephants and find themselves sandwiched between their massive grey hulks. What they could easily tread on in the darkness was not to be contemplated in this desperate walk.

The others were now struggling up, stretching and bending themselves to loosen stiff joints.

"Ready?"

Sam and Lisa responded with a 'yes'. The boy merely placed himself behind Sam.

They set off, moving more slowly and cautiously than before. They started to pass through thicker bush, making it difficult to avoid the thorny branches that tore at their clothes and whipped at their faces. Sam kept them going in a straight line. He wanted to hit the main track and cross it before turning down towards the river crossing point.

He stopped the group.

"We should be coming to the road in about 15 minutes." he hissed. "We have to be extremely careful from now on. Keep close. Keep very quiet."

The investigative part of Lisa's brain registered, as it had on several other occasions since being rescued, that something wasn't quite as it should be. But what exactly was it that kept jarring? She frowned as she tried to concentrate. It all centred on Sam. First there was the obvious fact that he wasn't in the least bit deferential to Russell, his superior officer. Indeed, oddly, Russell seemed quite happy to take orders from him! It was true that his knowledge of the area was impressive but how did a Rhodesian guide acquire such detailed information? On top of that there was something strangely familiar about him which she could not place. But in the end she was just too exhausted, her nerves too close to the edge, to marshall her thoughts properly. The rest of her brain wasn't interested in delving into the facts. It didn't really matter. She was going home. That was all that counted.

She stopped thinking and meekly followed Seki as he resumed walking behind Sam but as they got closer to the river track, even she could not fail to register the unmistakable deep rumbling of heavy vehicles on the move. Sam waved the others to stop then signalling his intention, went on alone. Within ten minutes he was back.

"Well, what is it?"

"Trucks, dozens of them. All heading down towards the crossing."

CHAPTER EIGHT

"You reckon the camp's been found?"

"Must have been. I reckon they are getting ready to sweep the area in the morning."

The full implication of this pronouncement took a few moments to sink it. Russell spoke with undisguised frustration.

"Now what? We don't stand a cat in hells chance of getting across unseen!"

They heard rather than saw Lisa collapse. She sat down on the ground, the anti-climax deflating her so completely that she felt an overwhelming exhaustion take over. She was sure she would never move again.

Sam turned back to Russell.

"Well, this time of the year it is a risk, but I can take you to another crossing point further along the river. It is very little used – it is no good for boats – and can only be crossed in the dry season anyway. We should not meet any resistance there and could easily reach it by tomorrow night. Once the rains start, it is impassable, but with only a few rain storms up in the hills so far, we might be lucky. The run-off should not have affected the river yet. Anyway, it has to be your best chance."

Russell squatted down in front of Lisa.

"Did you hear that, Lisa?"

She dumbly nodded.

"Come on, we can't give up now."

She still stayed slumped on the ground. The boy, Seki, touched her gently on the shoulder. This tiny gesture stiffened Lisa's resolve. If the boy could do it, so could she! She held her arm out to Russell who hauled her to her feet. She gave Seki a quick pat on the head.

"Thanks, Seki."

They moved off back into the thick bush, melting quickly into its protecting cover and travelled for another hour until they were all too exhausted, mostly through disappointment, to continue. Through the hard painful trek that night, they had all been kept going by the thought that within a few more hours they would be safe. It had propelled them on when their feet had gone numb and their legs had hardly the strength left to move their bodies forward. Now it felt as if they had been offered paradise, only to have it snatched away from them at the very last moment. It left a bitter taste in all their mouths, even Sam's.

Russell woke to find Lisa once more snuggled up to him. He smiled for no reason. This time he was awake before anyone else. He gently disentangled himself from Lisa, who moaned softly as she was disturbed. He crawled out from under the low flat shrub they had used for protection in the night and looked about him. The sun was well up and already burning down relentlessly onto the landscape that seemed to be never ending – sparse grass, scattered woodland with thickets of thorn scrub in all directions as far as he could see. The previous night's disappointment was still palpable. To think, they could be home by now, sleeping in beds with sheets, hot food, cold beers on tap, baths.....

He rubbed his chin, the coarse stubble grating between his fingers and thumb. He had to stop thinking like that. He had to stay positive. They could all manage one more day as long as they kept their wits about them and kept out of trouble.

Sam, stretching and yawning, joined him.

"This is becoming a marathon!"

"And how!" Russell paused awkwardly, not knowing how to broach what was on his mind.

"Sam?"

"What?"

"I've been thinking."

Sam gave Russell his full attention.

"You know you don't have to travel any further with us. You've done more than enough already. You need only point us in the right direction. It's time you thought about your own safety."

Sam responded by placing his hand on Russell's shoulder and nodding in the direction of the two sleeping bodies.

"It is time to get the others up and moving. The further up the river road we go, the less chance of our meeting a searching patrol."

"Sam!"

But Sam had already turned away. He was touched that his friend, still far from safety himself, should be concerned for his welfare but for him there was no choice. He had promised to get Russell and the hostages back across the Zambesi and as long as the Spirits gave him breath, he would never go back on his given word. Anyway, he was confident he would have little trouble merging in with the Zambians once he was on his own.

The four breakfasted on the monotonous diet of the now none too fresh cold antelope and sadsza, washed down with water. The small dishevelled group tried to put a brave face on events as they started out on another long day of trekking, this time marching parallel to the main river road about two miles inland, but the air of forced bravado fooled no-one.

By mid-afternoon, Sam stopped them and searched for a suitable hiding place to settle down.

"I reckon we should now be about opposite the crossing point. I'll leave at dusk and check the area. If it's clear, you go straight across."

Sam's words made it sound so wonderfully easy. The air of pessimism that had shrouded them most of the day changed to one of almost light headed excitement as the belief that they really were at the end of the nightmare journey took hold.

They rested and at five, Sam left them.

"I'll probably be gone about an hour."

"Take care."

Sam touched his amulet. "The Spirits of the Ancestors have been with us so far!"

The grinning face disappeared. In his absence, a uneasy silence descended upon the remaining three. It made Russell's ears sing so loudly that he decided to risk speaking. Anything was better than everyone sitting in their own isolated world.

He cleared his throat, the cough seeming to shatter the air of deepening anxiety that had enveloped them. Lisa and Seki both turned their heads and looked expectantly at him.

"Er, sorry," he started awkwardly, "I didn't mean to startle you. It's just that I was wondering whether you feel able to tell me what happened to you after the mine blast?"

Lisa pushed her hand through her short bobbed hair. It felt a greasy tangled mess to her touch. Could she face remembering? Sadness shadowed her pale blue eyes.

"Well, there's not much to say really. We were driving to the South African base at Mana Pools, where I was due to make a report on the 'boys in the bush'. I had done a series of them during the previous ten days." She looked half apologetically at Russell. "Crap stuff really."

She again fiddled with her hair for a few seconds before resuming.

"Anyway, as we were travelling towards Mana Pools, the car in front of ours just disintegrated before our eyes. One minute it was merrily bumping along at forty miles an hour and the next, there was a tremendous explosion and the car was nothing more than a smoking heap of twisted .....” The pain Lisa felt as she recalled the scene was plainly evident.

“It’s all right. You don’t have to describe it further. My patrol passed the scene a couple of days ago so I saw the aftermath for myself. It looked a real mess.”

There was an attempt at a grateful smile before Lisa’s face clouded over again as she struggled with her words.

“The driver was killed outright and Blackie – that’s Blackie Schwartz our sound man – was badly injured. Bob was unhurt but was in deep shock.” Lisa looked pensive.

“Funny, you know, I’ve seen reports on the aftermath of one or two mine incidents in my time, but I realise now that they have never managed to convey the full horror of that unexpected suddenness and overwhelming violence squeezed into such a brief fragment of time.”

Russell could only nod his agreement. He knew to his cost the full destructive power of mines and lived with the danger on a daily basis. Lisa paused, gathering up her thoughts.

“Anyway, we were trying to get Bob into our car and see what we could do for Blackie when seemingly out of no-where several armed gunmen surrounded us. They shot Blackie as he sat helpless in the car. Our driver tried to run away and he, too, was shot. Then the leader spoke briefly to Daniel, that’s Seki’s Father. He yelled something abusive at him then had him bayonetted to death.” Her breathing quickened and her voice rose as she relived the horror. “Over and over they...”

“Traitor! He called my Father a traitor, a white man’s dog!”

Lisa stopped in mid sentence, startled to hear Seki speak. They had forgotten he was there. She felt distraught that the child had been carrying such harrowing thoughts in his head all this time and she had done nothing to comfort him. She had thought only of her own misery.

"Oh, Seki. I'm sorry. I shouldn't be talking like this. Reminding you of everything." She saw a tear roll down Seki's cheek and in a rush of sympathy for the boy, put her arms around him and drew him close.

"Your Father certainly wasn't a traitor, Seki. Never believe that. I am sure he was a good, kind man and you should be proud of him."

Seki wiped his face with his fingers then pulled away in embarrassment, sitting himself a little apart from the white people. He was a man now. He had to learn to behave like one.

Inwardly smiling at Seki's behaviour – he could well remember the adolescent horror at his own Mother fussing over him in front of others – Russell coaxed Lisa to continue.

"Can you say what happened next?"

"They tied Bob, Seki and myself up. When I tried to protest, the leader hit me across the face." She touched her cheek, remembering vividly the red hot sting as the blow struck her, causing tears to well up, much to the satisfaction of her assailant.

"He put a knife to my throat and told me not to speak again unless he asked me a question, otherwise he would cut my tongue out. He then had his men put nooses around our necks and they led us away." She instinctively fingered her cut and swollen neck as she remembered the first constriction to her throat as the noose bit into her flesh. Every stumble had made it worse and with her fear adding to her breathing difficulties, she had been sure she would die of asphyxiation. Russell too, had noticed her neck. He was worried, though he hoped that it did not show on his face for the wound looked ugly and badly infected. He cursed that his small field dressing and first aid kit were lying with his pack somewhere the other side of the river. Stupid of him not to have packed it in his kidney pouch! He turned his attention back to what Lisa was saying.

"They dragged and pushed us through the bush. It was terrible. They hardly stopped for a rest and we seemed to zig zag all the time. I don't know how we kept going." Again she fingered her throat and gave a short humourless laugh. "Well, I suppose I do really.

Once we stopped by a stream and they all drank and re-filled their bottles. I was so desperate for a drink, I asked if we could drink too and they allowed us to go into the stream. Do you know, as I knelt down, all I could think was 'I wonder if I'll catch bilharzia'. Isn't that stupid? I mean, there I was being carted off to god-knows-where and all I could think about was catching bilharzia!" They both allowed themselves a short laugh to ease the tension that had built up as Lisa recounted her story. A deep frown quickly replaced Lisa's smile.

"As I began to drink, a boot suddenly pressed itself onto the back of my head and forced me under the water. Up until then I naively thought that I had seen and suffered the most that anyone could, but I was wrong. It was so frightening. With my hands tied behind my back, I couldn't do anything to stop the boot keeping my head under water. I was positive then that I was going to drown. I can't describe to you how horrible those few seconds were. I couldn't hold my breath and began to choke then at the last moment, I was released. As I struggled to regain my balance they all mocked me saying things like 'has Ma-dam drunk enough? Would the Mem-sahib like another drink?" Lisa's voice rose with anger and bewilderment. "How could they do that?"

Russell reached out to her.

"Its all right. If you want to stop...."

She calmed herself, her voice returning to no more than a whisper.

"No. No, now that I've started, I feel the need to talk about it."

"If you're sure? There will be plenty of time to talk to someone when you get back home."

Lisa shook her head. "No. No, I'd like to tell you."

"Okay." He smiled encouragingly. "So, they marched you for two days?"

"Yes. After the first day, they released Seki and made him carry some of their baggage. They had several porters with them but they took a lot of gear, including the drink and cigarettes we were taking up to the SAP base, from our car and I think they needed an extra back. Then we came to what was obviously the Zambesi river. Up until then, I had managed to keep myself going with the thought that somebody must have discovered the cars and search parties sent out. As long as we were on the Rhodesian side, I knew we had a slim chance. Once or twice I was sure I heard helicopters in the distance, but when we crossed the river..." Her voice trailed off and she went into deep thought. Her shoulders rose and she let out a long sigh.

"Waiting to cross, we met up with another gang that had just come over...." She stopped abruptly as that niggling suspicion in her head finally exploded into horrifying certainty.

"Sam was one of them, wasn't he? I remember now! That's where I've seen him before. What in god's name are you doing, befriending a terrorist!"

Russell was cagey.

"In the circumstances, does it matter?"

Lisa felt Russell tense. Vulnerable, needing Russell if she wanted to survive, she didn't want to anger him. Her instinct sensed danger so she eased back the accusation in her voice.

"I just don't understand and yet you obviously trust him."

"Absolutely. I wouldn't have come here on my own otherwise, so without him, you wouldn't have been rescued. I think we should leave it at that for the time being."

Lisa nodded an automatic agreement, then the full implication of what Russell had just said hit her. Her perturbed state turned to utter astonishment.

"You're not supposed to be here are you? Of course not! No-one in authority would have let you come. I can see that now. I've had it in the back of my mind that something wasn't quite right. I mean, the fact that there was just you and your so-called guide." The true status of Russell and Sam's relationship caused Lisa great difficulty, yet even as she wanted to forthrightly condemn it, she had to accept that it was this inconceivable friendship that had been the instrument of her release from her cruel captors. For that she had to be thankful. Her pinched features became transformed by a warm, wide smile that made Russell feel very good.

"I guess I owe you a drink when we get back!"

"Careful, I'll hold you to that!"

They sat in companionable silence, enjoying the moment, then Lisa spoke.

"So why did you risk so much? Why did you come after us?"

"It's a long story." Russell held his hand up to stop Lisa from probing any further. It was too uncomfortable a subject and he didn't want to remember too clearly the trouble he would be in when they got back to safety. "One day I'll tell you if you're interested. Perhaps over that beer you're going to buy me, but for now I'd like to get back to you. What happened once you were in Zambia?"

"Well, we crossed the Zambesi in dug out canoes

belonging to the local fishermen. It was easy to guess that they were fishing boats because of the stench. We were forced to lie face down in the bottom which had, oh I don't know, two or three inches of stinking, stagnant bilge water in it. Once the boat started to move, it was impossible to keep your face clear of the foul, sloshing stuff. I hate to think how much I swallowed and I still don't know how I didn't vomit it all back up again.

We alighted from the boats just yards from what I took to be a Zambian Army post. I could see the lights and hear voices. I expected to be taken there but instead we were pushed away into the hinterland. I wanted to call out but couldn't find my voice. Bob tried but was hit to the ground. Soldiers did come out of the post but they just called out a few words of greetings to our captors then returned inside."

Lisa tugged at a strand of hair then proceeded to twirl it around her finger as she retreated into her own thoughts for a while.

"It was the end for Bob. I could see the hope die in him. He just gave up. The terrible thing was that he knew what was going to happen to him. Or at least, he knew he was going to die. The last words he spoke to me were 'I wish I'd had the good sense to run, at least I'd have been killed quickly.' I can't bear to think about what they did to him. How can anyone behave like that towards another human being? How?"

Distressed, she once more broke down, her body heaving, racked by sobs. Russell tried to console her and patiently waited for her to calm down. Catching her breath, she eventually continued.

"One good thing. Once we were in Zambia, the gang relaxed. They moved much, much slower and took our nooses off. We walked for two days, arriving at the camp clearing in the late afternoon. Once we were there, the porters set out the camp and disappeared. We were tied to a tree and the terrorists slept. In the morning, after they had eaten, they all had a heated discussion, about us I think, which ended with the leader and one other leaving. The remaining gang members started to drink the beer and whisky they had stolen from us. They drank the whisky as if it was water and got drunk very quickly. That was when they gathered round the tree." Unchecked tears began to fall down her cheeks. "They..... they started touching me and making sickening, lewd gestures. I thought I was going to be raped for sure but Bob told them to stop. He...he called them black bastards. What a stupid thing to do! It caused them to immediately turn their attention from me to him. They untied him and dragged him over to the other tree and started to torture him.... They cut his tongue out..... Then his eyes .... He was trying to protect me!" She ended in another body racking sob. "It's all my fault!"

Russell swallowed hard, his own picture of Bob Martin all too uncomfortably fresh in his mind. It was not an image he was likely to forget even with time. He could find no words to say to Lisa so simply embraced her and held her until the sobbing subsided.

"It's no good thinking like that, Lisa. You couldn't help what happened. Its best not to dwell on it."

"No, but every time I close my eyes..." She shuddered as she took a deep breath, forcing herself to move on. "I couldn't believe it when you came to our rescue. Come to think of it, I think I owe you more than one beer." The smile she gave Russell was weak but determined.

"That's more like it! You've been tremendously brave so far. You've got to keep going now."

The talk petered out. Growing ever more anxious, Russell checked his watch with what he hoped was a casual, unconcerned glance. Sam had been gone an hour and a half.

It was still another twenty minutes before he returned and when he did so, Russell could sense that something was terribly wrong.

CHAPTER NINE

Struggling to find his way in the dark with only a rising moon to aide him, Sam finally stumbled, exhausted into the makeshift camp.

"We have a problem – a big problem." he managed to splutter as he sat down. The beads of perspiration stuck his shirt uncomfortably to his back and despite knowing there were anxious faces peering at him, had to take a few moments respite to catch his breath before being able to continue. Slowly, feeling once more in control, he explained his bombshell of a remark.

"The whole roadway is one continual line of army lorries." He gave a short, mirthless laugh. "I suppose we should be flattered. Our 'friends' have been discovered and it has sparked off a panic. There are wild reports that the Rhodesian army has carried out a full scale invasion or at the very least, sent in an SAS party as a prelude to one. I caught up with some civilians who were fleeing the area. Apparently the Country is on full alert and the whole length of the Zambesi is being patrolled by troops." He ended with an obvious, but nevertheless, devastating observation. "There is no way we will get across until the panic has died down."

"Stupid bastards! Stupid, stupid bastards!" snapped Russell, hardly able to contain his growing frustration at the Zambians' actions.

Sam ignored the vehement outburst and continued in a steady, controlled voice. "The only thing we can do is to sit it out, but we will have to move inland to be safe. The troops are gradually fanning out and will undoubtedly get this far before long."

They all sat in stunned silence trying to digest the unwelcome news. Hopes dashed once again, a deep air of despondency fell over the group, the heavy stillness broken only by the sharp snapping of a twig Russell was absentmindedly breaking as he considered this new barrier to their freedom.

"How long, do you think, before the Zambians realise there's no invasion or raiding party?"

"Hard to say, but presumably some form of contact will be made between the two Governments and assurances given by the Rhodesians that our attack has nothing to do with them." Sam paused, offering a sharp look towards Russell. "Always assuming, of course, that the Rhodesians have not invaded and we just happen to have blundered right into the middle of it."

Even in such a dire situation as they were in, Russell could only laugh aloud at such an absurd suggestion.

"No way!"

"Okay. Okay." Sam conceded. "So then maybe three or four days before life returns to normal."

"You mean we've got to wander the bush for another three or more days?" Lisa's voice betrayed her despair.

Sam hunched up, eyes closed as he pondered their situation.

"Say the Zambian army give the area a thorough sweep. They are still unlikely to go into the bush for more than a day's march. It is the Zambesi itself they are concerned with. That means if we move inland for a day, we should be able to find a secure camp to hole up in and be fairly safe. As long as we can find somewhere accessible to water, I am sure we can hunt for food of some sort to keep us going. Rest up for two days, then come back again. When nothing major happens, the Army is bound to stand down its troops."

Russell stroked his chin as he looked up into the night sky. Would the expected rains wait another four days for them? He was sure the same worrying thought would be in Sam's mind too, but there was little point in airing their concern in front of Lisa. There was nothing they could do about it. Russell kept it simple.

"We don't really have much choice, Lisa. I for one don't fancy getting caught."

His voice sounded very strained as he spoke and caused Lisa to look searchingly at the man sitting next to her. His face, she knew, still rather endearingly showed streaks of black on his forehead and cheeks but in the half light emitted by the moon, all she could gauge from his careworn features was the weight of responsibility he so obviously felt for the safety of the whole group.

She nodded slowly, realising only too well what capture would mean for Russell – and possibly for Sam too. She gave an involuntary shudder. "I guess you're right. We don't have much choice but its just ..."

"I know. We all know."

There was nothing else to be said. They could do nothing until morning. Sam handed round his flask containing fresh water and shared out the last few scraps of food which everyone mechanically ate in wretched silence before settling down as best they could. They attempted to sleep but as the false dawn came up, they were happy to get themselves to their feet. It had been the worst night so far for everyone. Their tense and weary bodies had found no relief on the hard ground and the quiet of the night had been broken by continual tossing, turning and heavy sighing as the adults had tried to find a more comfortable spot to rest. It had been a futile exercise and by morning Sam, Russell and Lisa felt stiff and out of sorts with themselves and the world about them. Their blistered and bruised feet caused them to hobble as they began to trek once again and only Seki seemed physically fit, but he still had not spoken more than a few syllables since seeing his Father killed.

The four, eyes downcast, trudged into the hinterland. For hours the landscape seemed to stay the same, making them feel they were on some kind of giant treadmill so that despite all their effort, they were in fact standing still. To every corner of the horizon seemed nothing but endless, monotonous yellow, dry grass dotted with dark green splashes that were the thorn bushes and spindly trees, their only comfort, the lessening of the sun's strength as the late afternoon wore on.

As the daylight began to fade, Sam stopped and called out to the others.

"Look! There is a kopje ahead. It should make a good place to rest up for the night."

The other three looked towards where Sam was pointing. They could just make out the dark bulk of a group of rocks rising up from the plain, about a quarter of a mile ahead.

"Think you can make it?" Russell spoke encouragingly to Lisa.

"I guess so." The voice was a monotone. She had long ago mentally switched to auto pilot. It even hurt to think now.

Sam and the boy went ahead. As Russell, helping Lisa to go that extra few hundred yards, approached the massive rock structure, he could see the shadowy figure of Sam carefully inspecting the rocks, for if it made a good place for them to rest up, it would also be a perfect place for a lion or leopard. Sam reached the top.

"Okay. It is clear to come up."

Seki scrambled up the rocks within seconds.

"Okay, Lisa. Up you go."

Lisa stood rooted to the spot. Almost at the end of her endurance, the daunting mass of bare rocks piled on top of one another with sheer, smooth surfaces which appeared to have no easy foothold to climb, defeated her. Panic gripped her.

"How?"

"Hold on a minute." Russell swung himself up and without apparent effort climbed the first boulder, finding purchase where Lisa saw none. He then leaned down and gave her his arm.

"Come on, grab hold."

She did as she was told, using Russell's strength to pull herself up. They continued this way until they reached a saucer shaped plateau at the top. One slender, cone shaped boulder that seemed to be balanced precariously on the very edge, offered shelter and a place to rest their weary backs. Seki squatting down, peered round the bottom of the rock.

"Look!"

So quiet had he been over the last few days that when he spoke, it so startled the others that Sam and Russell immediately dropped onto their stomachs, rifles at the ready.

They slithered to either side of the plateau and scanned down the kopje to the floor some forty feet below. In the nebulous light emitted by the red setting sun, Sam's strained eyes painfully scrutinised the area, trying to spy any movement. He saw nothing.

"Where Seki! What did you see?"

"No, not down there. Here! It is the shadow of the rock making a shape."

Sam, tired and fraught, turned to admonish Seki for giving them such a scare but changed his mind as he saw the child's grinning delight as he pointed out towards the large mass of an escarpment on the far side of the valley. Still visible in the glow of the sunset were three jagged dark streaks etched down the depth of the massif.

Sam looked over his shoulder at Russell who

sheepishly grinned back as, to please Seki, he wriggled over to peer round the standing rock. As the sun sank below the skyline, its rays elongated the shadow of the standing rock until it looked like a long, black spear lying across the valley floor. In the dying rays, the shadow stretched itself until it seemed to touch the far escarpment, the spear head pointing exactly to the middle scar. Simultaneously Sam and Russell's pulses began to quicken.

"You reckon those dark lines are valleys, Sam?"

"Definitely."

Russell rubbed his red, smarting eyes. It wasn't only his pulse that was racing. His thoughts seemed out of control too! He whispered, almost to himself.

"The Valley of the Black Spear!" But could they seriously have stumbled upon the hiding place of the King's treasure?

He shook his head to disown his own thoughts. No. He was being more than just stupid now.

"Tell me I've finally cracked and started to hallucinate Sam!" He turned his head towards his friend to seek reassurance but Sam's face mirrored his own wide-eyed agitation. They both silently looked back towards the horizon. Within a minute, the sun had become just a thin red rim across the sky line and the shadowy spear disappeared.

"What do you think? How far is it from here?" Russell spoke in a conspiratorial murmur and Sam replied in the same vein.

"Five miles?"

"Yeah.... We could make it in a morning's walk."

"No problem."

"Hey, you guys, what are you whispering about?" Lisa, her back propped up against the standing stone and eyes closed in exhaustion, had not bothered to see what had caused Seki to call out. As long as it wasn't dangerous, she didn't care! With no energy left at all, even curiosity could not move her.

The two men exchanged glances. Sam made a small shaking motion of his head and Russell answered Lisa's question as casually as he could through a mounting excitement inside him, an excitement he knew to be quite unfounded.

"There's an escarpment about five miles from here. A morning's easy walk. It looks as if it might be a good place to hide out."

"Do you promise it will only take a morning to get there?"

"Yes."

Lisa and Seki curled up and slept but the two men sat side by side in the darkness, speaking in low whispers.

"Its a pretty long shot that this is the place, Sam."

"Maybe, but it makes sense of all that I have been told about the secret place and the shadow of the Black Spear showing the way. I never understood it before. It had always seemed so vague. Now ...." He left the sentence unfinished, the word hanging in the air between them. When his Father had first placed the amulet around his neck, Sam had been very conscious of its importance and revered it, but gradually over the years, it had lost its significance and most of the time he was not even aware that he was wearing it. But tonight the amulet burnt hotly into his skin. It demanded attention. When he spoke again, Sam sounded more positive. "Anyway, I do know that it is roughly in the right area, so it could be." His voice stressed the 'could'.

'What you mean' Russell interpreted in his own head, *'is that, just like me, you want it to be.'* He said nothing out loud for a while, deep in his own thoughts, trying to curb the sense of anticipation that had built up since seeing the thin shadow briefly yet so dramatically sign post the way. It was so little to go on

and yet no matter how hard he tried to apply cold logic to the situation, he could not dismiss the idea from his mind. After all, he admitted, going off in search of a lost treasure trove might be pretty idiotic but it wouldn't be the first foolhardy thing he had done recently.

"Well, we'll find out tomorrow so I guess we'd better get some sleep. Good night Sam."

"Good night."

It took all morning to get to the escarpment. From the top of the kopje the intervening bush country had looked flat and easy, the grass gently rippling in the light breeze, but when they started to walk through it, the area was undulating with several small valleys, all blanketed with low thorn scrub that tore at their trousers and scratched their legs. There were few game trails to follow, making progress very slow and painful.

Setting their sights on the middle valley, they walked on. At first, the escarpment seemed to stay a distant purple haze, the valley just a thin dark scar on its lower face but as the sun reached its zenith, the struggling group's progress was visibly rewarded. At last they could make out individual trees and features on the towering scarp now stretching across their whole horizon which close to, was scarred by many valleys and plateaux as it rose majestically above them.

They paused to get their bearings at a river whose origins seemed to come from the valley they were seeking. Its beds were sun-baked and cracked, its water hardly more than a trickle after the long dry season it had endured.

The group walked in the river, the cool of the water easing the pain in their aching, swollen feet. They followed its meandering route back to the mouth of the middle valley which was formed by two shoulders extending from the main body of the massif like embracing arms, leaving a narrow gap through which the river ran. As they walked through the gap, dwarfed by the height of their surroundings, they seemed to enter another world. Protected by the tree covered shoulders and fed by the stream, lush vegetation grew in stark contrast to the yellow, parched grass of the savannah they had just left. A cool, oppressive stillness seemed to shroud them and Lisa shivered at the change in temperature.

About a hundred yards into the valley, the shoulders widened out into a large bowl, the river ending in a small pool formed from the power of the free falling water that tumbled over a ledge forty or fifty feet above them.

Lisa thankfully knelt down and splashed the refreshing cold water onto her face before indulging in a long drink. The men followed her example before exploring the area further.

Sam went to the left with Seki and Russell scouted to his right as Lisa found a small mound amongst the vegetation and sat gratefully down upon it. It did not take the men long to return to the river for the gorge seemed to come to a dead end at the waterfall face. They craned their necks to look up at the ledge above them. Although it extended the length of the rock wall in front of them, there seemed no way of getting to the top and in any event, a sheer rock wall continued to rise above it.

"What do you think?"

Sam stroked his chin.

"I think we have stumbled on an ancient burial ground."

"What!" Lisa leapt to her feet, looking in horror at the mound she had been sitting on. "Do you mean I've been sitting on someone's grave?"

A mischievous smile spread over Sam's face.

"Yes."

"Ugh!" Lisa shuddered and moved closer to Russell.

"You can see many such mounds hidden by the undergrowth if you look. I'm certain, Russell, it is a burial ground, but by the state of it, it has long since been abandoned."

"So where does that leave us?"

"I don't know. I cannot see any way of getting out of here other than the way we came in."

"Damn!" Disappointment nearly choked Russell. "Is there any point in us camping here anyway?"

"I'm not sleeping in a grave yard!" Lisa's eyes flashed some of their normal assertiveness.

"Well if we don't ......"

Sam stopped in mid sentence as an echoing call had the three of them looking up. They gaped in unison. Seki was standing on the ledge.

"Seki! Seki get down from there at once before you fall!" shrieked Lisa.

"Stay where you are Seki!" countered the men. "Tell us how you got up there."

Seki pointed down below him.

"Footholds on the wall." He shouted back, pleased with himself that he had discovered something the adults had not.

Confounded, Sam and Russell looked at one another for a brief second before crashing through the vegetation.

"Where? I can't see anything, Sam."

"Neither can I"

The two men frantically scoured the wall.

"Yes! Here!" Just above his reach, Russell pointed to a hollow in the rock so artfully sculpted to blend with its surroundings that an unsuspecting eye would mistake it for just another natural niche in the rock and dismiss it. But careful exploration revealed several such notches all the way up the face of the wall. He cleared away some of the vegetation at the base of the wall and three feet up, another hollow showed itself.

Sam was already scrambling up the wall.

"Do you want to stay here while we explore, Lisa?"

Lisa dreaded the thought of scaling the wall. If she fell.... but she did not relish the idea of being left alone amongst the graves either.

"I....I...." She gulped. "I don't know that I can manage it, Russ."

"Sure you can. And I'll be right behind you." He gently pushed her to the wall. "Go on, you'll be all right."

Lisa took a deep breath then stood on the first two footholds and with trembling fingers reached out to the hollow above her. It gave a reassuring grip. Russell shouted instructions.

"Good. Now start climbing and remember the golden rule. Don't look down."

To her surprise, the footholds made the assent much easier than she had feared and she felt a surge of achievement as she gained the top. It was quickly dispelled as she looked about her. The rock face they were resting against rose a hundred feet vertically above them and the ten foot wide ledge they were on took them no-where, offering only a magnificent panoramic view of the vast African plain below them. She had risked death for nothing more than a spectacular view!

Russell and Sam proceeded to confer in whispers as they examined their surroundings. Their behaviour was beginning to worry Lisa. They had started to act very strangely and either they were suffering from sun stroke or they knew something she did not.

"Just what are you two looking for?"

Sam, deep in concentration, spoke without thinking.

"Some form of opening."

"A what?"

Sam turned round, an exasperated look on his face. He didn't need questions being fired at him at that moment. Just in time, he realised that their behaviour would make no sense to an outsider and his face relaxed as he attempted to fend off Lisa's curiosity.

"Look, we will explain it all to you if we find some way forward but, please, just rest for the moment. Seki, stay with Miss Barnard."

Lisa slithered to the ground, hardly mollified by Sam's explanation. She watched bemused as Sam turned back to examining the rock wall.

It was no good, he conceded. They had been wrong. This was just an ordinary rock formation, one of many thousands dotted across the African landscape. He felt a terrible sense of anti-climax.

"I think we are wasting our time Russell. This wall really is impossible to climb."

"Maybe, but I just want to check something out."

Sam squatted down and watched as Russell carefully made his way across the waterfall to the far end of the ledge which was blocked by a rock fall. A large slab of rock had pulled away from the main cliff, creating a deep fissure. Russell clambered over the rubble at the base and disappeared. Moments later his head re-appeared.

"Sam!"

Sam was at the boulders within seconds, Lisa and Seki hot on his heels. Russell's face was flushed with excitement.

"In here. Quick!"

The three scrambled over the rubble and followed Russell as he led the way into a small cave, concealed from below by the broken rock. Russell shone his torch against the wall and illuminated ancient bushmen's paintings.

"Wow!" was all Lisa could say as the beam of light

arced around the walls.

Russell nudged Sam and they moved to the back of the cave. "And look. Feel this."

Sam bent down to a small triangular cleft and put his hand against it. A slight breeze wafted over his hand. He put his face against the hole.

"Fresh air!"

"That's what I thought." Russell dropped his webbing and kidney pouch to the floor and handed his rifle to Sam before flattening himself on the ground and wriggling his way through the gap that was barely large enough for a man to get through.

"Watch it Russell! If you get stuck, we will never be able to pull you out!"

There was no reply as, to the consternation of the others, Russell's body began to disappear, inch by inch, into the hole. When only his legs below the knees were still visible, the shuffling stopped then after a moment, reversed. The three watchers felt the relief wash through them as his body re-emerged.

"Well?" Sam's face showed his rising excitement.

"I think this may be something."

Sam let out a whoop and jumped, punching the air in exhilaration, causing Lisa some anxiety.

"Will you two PLEASE tell me what's going on!"

"In a minute."

"That's what Sam said half an hour ago."

"Okay, okay. I know we seem to be behaving oddly but we've just got to find out where this tunnel goes. You can stay here if you want."

"Not bloody likely!" she exploded. "The way you two are acting at the moment, you might forget to come back. Seki and I are coming with you. Right, Seki?"

The boy nodded.

"Fair enough." Russell turned to Sam. "Once you've squeezed past the first few yards of the tunnel, it seems to change to a steeply stepped passageway. I can't make it out clearly but it seems to open out a little way ahead, so I'm going to go as far as I can. Give me five minutes."

He took back his rifle and scooped up his belongings from the cave floor and with that he was once more wriggling through the tiny gap. The rest stood in silence, Sam's eyes glued to his watch. One, two, three, four, five interminable minutes passed. He bent down to the gap.

"Russell, can you hear me?"

A muffled voice answered.

"Yes. Come on through."

Sam stood up.

"Do you want me to go next?"

"No!" The answer from Lisa was emphatic. She was not prepared to have Seki and herself left alone in this spooky cave, even for five minutes. "I think Seki should go next, then me and you last."

Sam bit back his own impatience and nodded to Seki who immediately began to wriggle through the gap, quickly followed by Lisa. Finally Sam could start his journey through the hole. It was pitch black but he could see a faint light ahead and inched his way towards it, pushing his pack and rifle ahead of him. The A.K. scraped along the rock as the tunnel suddenly gave way to a steep staircase, so narrow that Sam had to turn himself sideways to advance. The roof pressed down on him making it even more difficult to move. He felt claustrophobic. He felt alone. He felt trapped and fought to control the feeling of panic rising within him.

"Are you okay Sam? It's a tight squeeze." The dim light shone more brightly as Russell directed his torch down the passageway.

"I'm fine." Sam managed to call out, the fear evaporating as he clambered up the last step onto a circular landing where the others were waiting. Like the passageway itself, it was clear that this had been painstakingly hewn out of the rock. It was small, its circumference no more than eight foot across, its roof still only a hair's breath above Sam when he stood upright. In the dim light emitted by the torch another flight of steep narrow steps could be seen disappearing into the darkness ahead.

Without another word, Russell proceeded to climb, everyone else following in line. Twenty steps were negotiated before reaching another landing and although the travellers were grateful for the chance to regain their breath, Russell doubted that a handy resting place was the true purpose of the levels.

"What do you think, Sam?"

Sam looked into the darkness behind him and into the darkness in front where another flight of steps awaited them.

"I reckon this is a fighting corridor. These levels could be defensive stands. Just one man standing alone in these positions could easily fend off intruders especially as anyone attempting to negotiate the passageway would be greatly hindered in the use of their weapons by its narrowness."

"Is it safe to go on?" Lisa whispered anxiously. She was not enjoying the exploration of the passageway. Apart from the cold and the forbidding darkness, her arms kept painfully scrapping against the sharp edges of the rock as she used them to help haul herself up the steep incline. She would happily return to the grave yard.

"Of course its safe." Russell had no intention of going back now. These steps had to lead to somewhere and that somewhere had to be important for all this labour to have been expended. "But if you want to take the torch and go back..."

"No." came the miserable reply.

"Then lets climb the next flight of steps and see where that takes us."

It took them to yet another landing and another set of steps. Sam, beads of cold sweat on his face, struggled up the last few feet as the blackness finally gave way to an eerie light. As he looked around him in amazement, he found himself standing at the back of yet another cavern, but this time large enough for many people to gather. Russell, Lisa and Seki were standing huddled together staring towards the large opening at the far end. Strong shafts of sunlight flooded in, clearly illuminating the obstacle that prevented them from reaching their goal. There, braced diagonally across the centre of the cave were two massive spears, from which hung a baboon skull and the long black tail feathers of the widow bird now gently fluttering in the slight breeze.

CHAPTER TEN

"What is it Sam, any idea?"

Sam certainly did have an idea. He recognised the intricate cobra carvings on the shaft of the spears and understood the meaning of the skull and feathers. They were there to warn that a powerful spell had been cast – and that dire consequences would befall anyone foolish enough not to heed it. But before he could speak and, as if in answer to the question, a shadowy figure appeared in the opening of the cave. His features were obscured by the strong sunlight behind him but the stabbing assegai he held ready in his hand was clearly visible. A deep, resonant voice spoke sharply to them in a language Russell could not place.

"He says 'Whosoever crosses the spears uninvited, seeks death'."

Russell was immensely relieved to hear Sam translate. At least one of them would be able to understand and communicate that they had come with peaceful intentions.

"How do you know what he said?" It was Lisa who spoke, now totally confused by the events overtaking her.

"He's speaking a local dialect from the Zambian tribes around here. I picked it up during my stay."

Russell tried to ignore the daggered look that was directed at him by Lisa as she understood the implications of Sam's words.

The shadowy figure had not moved, nor did it seem that he was going to speak again.

Sam cleared his throat and took two steps forward before halting as the stance of the wary guard shifted ominously in response. Sam held up his hands in a gesture of submission.

"We come as holders of the Sacred Amulets." He cautiously brought his right hand down and pulled his pendant out of his shirt. He glanced across at Russell and motioned him to do the same.

"Look!"

The guard studied first Sam and then more warily, Russell.

"What is your name?" he asked Sam.

"I am Sam, son of Nyati, whose forefather was one of the chosen two hundred."

The figure nodded and then beckoned the party forward. He called out as they went to move around the spears.

Sam yanked Lisa back.

"Wait! The guardian says we must go through the centre of the spears otherwise we will set off trip wires hidden by the loose earth. We should walk in single file."

Sam went first, followed by Seki and Lisa who shuddered in revulsion as she walked under the baboon skull. Russell was 'tail end Charlie' and as he walked he looked up to the ceiling of the cave. There, suspended above him was a network of weighted spears ready to shower down on anyone foolish enough to spring the trap. He trod very carefully down the centre of the cave and moved into the sunlight to join the others.

Blinking in the strong glare, they found themselves standing on another ledge. Lisa clung to Russell's arm as he risked a quick glance over the edge. There, twenty feet below the sheer drop, appeared a tantalisingly green and fertile oasis.

The ledge they were perched on narrowed to a path that disappeared between more rocks and it was here that the African, dressed only in a red loin cloth, stood. Russell reckoned the man was at least sixty but despite the grey hair, he presented a formidable figure.

Deeply suspicious and threatening with the assegai still poised to attack, the man spoke curtly to Sam.

"He wants to see our amulets again."

The African beckoned Sam forward and took the proffered amulet in his hand. He carefully examined the pendant before scanning Sam's face with such intensity that Sam blinked in discomfort.

"I am Sam, son of Nyati, whose forefather was one of the chosen two hundred." he repeated.

The old man nodded slowly. He knew the names of all the two hundred. He beckoned Russell. Lisa tightened her grip, reluctant to let Russell go.

"It will be all right. Just stay here and stay calm." He disentangled himself and moved forward, acutely aware of the hostile mistrust on the part of the old African because of his white face. He looked across to Sam and just hoped that he could reassure this guardian of the treasure – for Russell was now convinced that they really had stumbled upon the ancient treasure trove – that they posed no threat. The African pointed at Russell, demanding to hear him speak.

"Sam, please tell him that an African called Mukora, who lived in Kenya, gave the amulet to me as a boy. He was my friend but was old and without any living relatives. Before he died, he gave the amulet to me for safe keeping."

The African's features continued to remain totally impassive but inwardly he was perplexed. The Spirits had forewarned him he would shortly receive a visit from one of the descendants but he had never imagined he would be faced with a group that included a white man and woman, one of whom looked extremely haggard and the other as if she was about to collapse at any moment. Although he had made no show of noticing Seki, he had nevertheless seen the boy and his presence helped reassure him.

However, he had to be absolutely sure that the white man was telling the truth and was not a threat to the King's Treasure House. Without removing his eyes from Russell's face, he spoke again.

"He wants to know exactly what this Mukora told you."

Russell looked straight into the eyes of the old African, aware that, as the window to a man's soul, it was his eyes, as much as his words, that the African was scrutinising. He then repeated as closely as he could that last conversation he had had with Mukora.

The African thought for a while as he digested Sam's translation. Surely if the amulet had been stolen or taken by force, the history of the Kingdom would not be known. The white man's eyes held no guile. He was satisfied and gave a small nod as he turned down the path and motioned them to follow.

Lisa standing well back and so unable to hear clearly what was being said by the men was visibly agitated.

"Will someone please tell me what's going on!" she squealed. "And don't tell me 'later'!"

"Later!" chorused Sam and Russell as they started off after the African.

Realising she was not going to get any sense out of the men, Lisa turned to Seki, but he merely raised his shoulders and spread out his arms in an uncomprehending gesture before passively following Sam. Hot, bothered, tired, irritated, yet immensely curious, Lisa had no option but to join the men as they carefully made their way forward.

The path between the rocks would only permit single file as it led them through a corridor where the afternoon sun struggled to penetrate the deep fissures. They moved in a long downward spiral and as they rounded the last boulder, gasped in amazement as they found themselves on the edge of a natural amphitheatre.

The cleared flat area was completely surrounded and protected by the rocks and cliffs on which several massive fig trees grew, their root systems tumbling down to the ground in masses of twisting thick plaits. Interspersed with the lush green foliage of the figs, were tall, grey barked acacias, their flat spreading branches making a filigree of fine foliage that camouflaged the amphitheatre from above while still allowing the sunlight to filter down and offer dappled shade to the miniature world below.

To their left there was a large cave which seemed to be where the African lived and across the open area of grass, nibbled down to a fine lawn by a few tethered goats, a deep pool glistened. Its waters were being constantly replenished by a spectacular cascade of water that fell sixty feet down the face of the protecting cliff towering above the pool and the sound of the waterfall's crystal clear droplets tumbling into the pool magically lifted the fatigue from the mesmerised onlookers. The rocks, nourished by the spray, had their natural bareness voluptuously covered by ferns, lichens and mosses and Russell knew if he looked carefully, he would spot a Mother of Pearl butterfly living somewhere in this garden of Eden where the air was alive with bird song and the hum of a myriad insects.

The African led the group to the fire outside the cave and invited them to sit. Almost overwhelmed at the realisation that they could finally completely relax, they collapsed onto the grass. The African went into his cave and came back carrying a tin tray holding four enamel mugs, chipped with age. He proceeded to fill the mugs with steaming liquid taken from a pot on the fire, carefully stirring each one before offering a mug in turn to Sam, Russell, Seki then Lisa. To everyone's surprise and delight, the mugs held hot, black tea sweetened with honey. It tasted wonderful.

The old man smiled more benignly now. Politeness demanded that he ask no immediate questions as to how this strange assortment of people had come to descend upon him but instead played host to his unexpected visitors with calm and hospitable dignity. He returned once again to the dark recess of the cave and this time came back carrying a pile of gaudily printed cloth, topped with a bar of soap. Smiling politely, he motioned to the pool and took the bundle down to the edge of the water.

Made aware of their dishevelled state, Sam and Russell gladly stripped off their clothes and dived into the cool refreshing water. Before long they were laughing and splashing each other with childish glee.

"Come on Lisa. Its terrific!"

"I'll let you two go first. I'll just sit and paddle my feet for a while."

Sitting on a small rock, she eased her boots off. Her white socks were coloured a mixture of dark dirt brown and blood red and seemed permanently stuck to the soles of her feet. She gingerly dipped her feet into the cold water hoping it would help release the socks from her skin and watched fascinated as the water turned deep pink. After a few minutes, she raised her feet out of the water. She eased the sock tops over her heels then holding her breath, she simultaneously yanked the socks off both feet in one quick movement causing herself to nearly faint with the pain. She was convinced that she had pulled a whole layer of skin off her soles but fearing what she would see, chose not to look. Carefully lowering her torn and bleeding feet back into the cold water, there was an almost instant easing of the throbbing that had been her constant companion since being forced through the bush by her captors.

Lisa sat, moving her legs in a gentle arcing

movement, allowing the peace and tranquillity of this strangely beautiful place to wash over her as with almost matriarchal indulgence, she watched the two laughing men swimming in the deep sparkling water. She didn't know where she was or why they had come here, but it offered such a welcome respite from the hardship she had suffered over the past few days that she was content for the moment not to seek an explanation.

Seki, who had stayed with the old African, came down to the water's edge and gathered Sam and Russell's clothes. He gave a shy smile to Lisa, who with idle curiosity watched as he went to the spot where the water flowed out from the pool and disappeared through a crevice in the rocks on its journey down to the floor of the valley and the river. There, making use of a large smooth stone obviously placed there for the purpose, he began to wash the clothes.

Russell cheerily called across to Lisa, breaking the spell.

"Close your eyes, we're coming out!"

He and Sam quickly wound the lengths of material around their bodies in the fashion of sarongs. Russell checked his swollen and blistered feet, once more cursing himself for putting the indispensable tube of antiseptic cream into his pack rather than his kidney pouch. Some of his blisters looked particularly angry.

He heard a splash behind him and turned to see Lisa in the water.

"Doesn't that feel good?"

"Fabulous!"

He sauntered across the grass and joined the old African who was squatting by the fire stirring the contents of a large pot sitting on the three firestones, The smell of cooking meat began to waft into Russell's nostrils reminding him of how hungry he was. His mouth salivated in anticipation.

Sam stood a little to the side of the open cave, busy shaving. When he had finished, he offered the borrowed and ancient safety razor to Russell, who shook his head.

"No. Thanks. I think I'll stay as I am." He fingered his face. His stubble was now growing into a beard which he fancied rather suited him, so he decided against the use of a razor – at least until he got back to his Station. Apart from being against regulations, Makesmith would certainly not entertain the idea of him keeping it. Beards, Makesmith had once disparagingly pronounced in his hearing, were only for the chinless wonders with something to hide. The sudden, unwelcome spectre of Makesmith rising up in front of him caused Russell's stomach to knot painfully in an acute panic attack. During the excitement of the previous 24 hours, he had completely forgotten about Rhodesia, Zambia and all the problems his rashness in crossing the Zambesi had caused him. Now determinedly swallowing down the lump in his throat, Russell remonstrated with himself. It was no good worrying about tomorrow. He had found his way to Eden and the only thing he could do now was to enjoy it to the full.

A sharp cry of distress from behind him brought Russell out of his reverie. Concerned, he turned towards Lisa.

She had already come out of the water and wrapped her piece of cloth around her body in a fetching sarong. But now she was sitting, huddled into a ball, cradling one of her feet in her hands, tears of pain trickling down her cheek.

"Here, let me." Russell crossed the short space between them and easily swung her up into his arms. Lisa gratefully rested her head on Russell's shoulder and let him carry her to the camp fire.

No sooner had he done so than the old African came forward and meticulously examined Lisa's feet and neck, now seeping yellow puss and showing signs of heavy infection.

He reassuringly patted her shoulder then walked to the far shore of the pool where he gathered a bunch of large leaves from one of the waterside plants. Placing them carefully by Lisa's feet, he then collected from the cave two clay pots from which he extracted some crushed dried berries and powders which he mixed together in a bowl with a little water. Continuing to work in an unhurried fashion, he spread the paste onto the leaves before binding them around Lisa's feet with strips of torn cloth. He then very gently spread some more of the medicine around Lisa's neck, the smell of which was so appalling that she reeled back in disgust. The African grinned and nodded as if to say he understood her reaction. He spoke briefly to Sam who had rejoined the group.

"Dume, that's our host's name by the way, says that if you wear this poultice for three days your wounds will heal without trace."

Lisa was rigid. She didn't like the African rubbing this unknown medicine, the strong smell of which made her feel quite sick, into her wounds. Who knew what it was made from? It could make matters worse. But she realised that to refuse would greatly offend and possibly cause the African – what was his name? – yes, Dume, to cast them out. She summoned up a weak smile.

"Please thank Dume for me. I...I feel better already." she lied.

Russell's feet were then examined. He had blisters on his toes but his heels had become ulcerous where blister upon blister had formed then burst. Dume held the bowl towards Russell, who took a finger full of the mixture and applied it to his heels. It felt cold on impact but within minutes began to make his heels feel pleasantly warm.

As the sun lost its strength, Seki collected the clothes that had been left to dry on the boulders, including Lisa's that she had washed herself, and took them into the cave, placing them in neat piles at the bottom of three rush mattresses covered with hyrax fur karosses.

The day's work complete, Dume served up the staple maize meal porridge of sadsza with the stew. For once, Lisa was not concerned to know what kind of meat was in the stew, it just felt marvellous to be eating hot food again.

Sitting by the light of the fire, replete after their meal and enjoying the luxury of drinking mugs of tea, Dume finally judged it polite to ask about his guests. Were Russell and Lisa, man and wife?

Sam was prepared to answer Dume's questions as fully as he was able but at this absurd idea, fell into fits of uncontrollable laughter, choking himself as he attempted to translate Dume's question to Russell and Lisa. The two, puzzled by this outburst from Sam, were somewhat put out at this obvious joke at their expense, for it hadn't gone unnoticed that Seki, too, was giggling behind his hand, but finally Sam had enough control over himself to explain what Dume had asked. Lisa and Russell looked at one another and shrugged, still baffled as to why such a reasonable suggestion on the part of Dume should cause Sam and Seki such mirth.

"So? So what's so funny about that?"

Sam, his words still punctuated with laughter, apologised.

"Sorry Russell.....Lisa .... It is just that ..... I, I don't know really." he finished lamely, only aware of how good it felt to laugh again. "It just struck me as funny thats all." Another bout of laughter caught him as he spoke. It was infectious making everyone join in.

Using his upper arms to wipe the tears from his face, Sam tried to explain to Dume about his and Russell's meeting. How they had decided to attempt a rescue of Lisa and Seki and how, afterwards, finding themselves unable to cross the Zambesi they moved inland instead, finally resting at the kopje from which they recognised the shadow of the black spear which brought them to this place.

Dume listened intently throughout the long explanation. He showed no sign of surprise at the strange turn of events being related to him and at the end merely nodded wisely, remarking only upon the fact that the Spirits of the Ancestors moved in mysterious ways, before suggesting that it was late, the company tired and it was time to sleep.

It suited everyone. Sam went into the cave but before Lisa could struggle to her feet, Russell bent down and once more picked her up.

"Oh no you don't. You're not to walk on your feet for at least a day."

He carried her into the cave, the movement of his body making Lisa only too aware of his masculinity. She was settled down on the middle mat.

"Welcome to the Zambesi Meikles!" he jested, "We hope you will enjoy your stay here."

Lisa sank into the luxury of the kaross.

"Oh what bliss! Hey, what's that?" She shifted her weight as something hard dug into her backside. Fumbling beneath her, she pulled out an object and although she could not make out the details in the darkness of the cave, she could feel the mass of tiny decorative carvings on its spine.

Lisa laughed in delight.

"A comb. How wonderful! Dume seems to have thought of everything." She pulled the comb through her tangled mop as she turned to Russell, her voice turning to silk. "And you, too. You're spoiling me."

A flush of pleasure coloured his cheeks. He stretched out on his mattress, thankful for the cover of darkness but as he closed his eyes, a thought struck him and he sat up.

"Where's Seki?"

The sleepy, muffled voice of Sam answered.

"With Dume. They are sleeping outside by the fire."

"Have you noticed how happy Seki seems to be since we got here?"

"Yes. Now, please, be quiet and go to sleep."

Sam turned over, facing the wall, his back to the others and Russell did the same. Lisa lay awake listening to the steady rhythm of Russell's breathing. She had the strongest urge to snuggle up into the comforting curve of his body, but the constant putrid smell of the paste around her neck stopped her from reaching out to him.

Instead, revelling in the luxury of the bed, she at last speculated about the weird events happening around her. Why was Sam, a man who by definition must hate the whites, helping her? What was the true nature of his relationship with Russell? It had something to do with those strange pendants but what? She turned her head towards the recumbent body of Russell. The evenness of his breathing convinced her that he was asleep. Knowing there would be no answers until the following day she began to mull over the mystery of Russell himself. He must have disobeyed orders to find her. Why had he risked so much? She realised with something of a start that when it came to it, she knew absolutely nothing about him, other than his name. Even that could be false. She had taken him at face value, accepted without proof that he really did serve in the BSAP. But he could be anybody – in the darkness, blind panic started to rise within her – even a kidnapper! This place could be their hideaway. They ....

No! She calmed herself. She was being hysterical from tiredness and stress. She had always trusted her instincts and she was confident that after the experience they had shared over the last few days, she had not misjudged Russell's character. Besides, now with that ridiculous dye washed off his face, he was disarmingly attractive – or was it just that her feelings were distorted simply because she knew she was totally dependent upon him? It was all too confusing.

The words of Dume came to mind and she began to wonder what it would be like to be held in Russell's arms not in comfort but in passion. The thought caused a butterfly sensation of excitement to start in the pit of her stomach. The reaction settled her mind that one day she would find out but then drowsiness took over and she fell into the deep sleep of someone who had not a care in the world.

She awoke slowly, aware that someone was shaking her and softly calling her name. A face materialised out of the foggy sleepiness. It was Russell.

"Come on sleepy head. Time to be transported outside." He lifted her from the bed, surprised as he had been yesterday as to how light she was.

He took her to the edge of the water and retreated back to the camp fire as she washed herself. She hobbled back and sat down, ready for a mug of tea.

"Aren't you going inside to change?" Russell was back to wearing his fatigues.

"No, I think I'll continue to wear my sarong. It seems to go with the feeling I have of being stranded in paradise."

Russell chuckled.

"I know what you mean. Can't help thinking that the Garden of Eden must have been something like this."

He handed her a mug of tea. She noticed a bowl of medicine and fresh leaves on the ground. Whilst she sipped the refreshing liquid, Russell administered to her feet.

"Bloody hell, Lisa! That's amazing. Your feet really do look a lot better."

"Do they?"

"Yes! Mind you, I think the smell alone would knock any germs for six!"

"It is a bit violent, isn't it!" She wrinkled her nose up in revulsion as the smell of the fresh medicine reached her. She paused, wondering whether now was the right time to demand an answer to the question that had been left hanging in the air since she had watched Russell and Sam look for the opening in the rocks.

"Russ.... what's going on?"

"Let me finish this, and I'll tell you a story." He completed the fresh dressing around her neck. Again the yellow puss had miraculously receded and the angry red skin had begun to fade down to a healthier pink.

"I really think you will be better in a couple of days. Look at my heels, they're almost back to normal." Russell applied the left over mixture to his own heels. "Get the recipe for this, find a way of disguising the smell and we'd be made for life!"

"That's a great idea!" She laughed, then locked her clear, inquisitive eyes onto his, determined this time not to be side tracked away from her question. "So, okay, what's going on? And don't give me 'later'." She looked around her. "By the way, where have the others got to?"

"Dume has taken Seki off to help him and Sam's over there behind the rocks. I got the feeling that he wanted to be alone with his own thoughts for a while. As for what's going on, well, I have to have your solemn promise that what I'm about to say will go no further than between ourselves."

"That sounds ominous. Surely it's not as serious as all that?"

"Yes it is. And I have to have your word."

Lisa ran her hand through her hair as she weighed up what Russell had said. She had not truly anticipated a real story to come out of this, expecting some quite boring, rational explanation that disappointed, but now her finely honed journalist's nose smelt a big scoop. She realised it was this that Russell – and presumably Sam and Dume – were afraid of.

"You mean I can't write up a story for the TV or newspapers?"

"I mean you are to say nothing at all to anyone."

"Oh come on, Russ, thats a bit steep! In heavens name why not? What on earth is there to be so secretive about?"

"Give me your word and I'll tell you."

Lisa thought long and hard. In the end, she knew that Russell would not speak without her pledge of secrecy. He and Sam knew something very strange, possibly even dangerous and in telling her at all, they were placing a great deal of trust in her not to speak out when they returned home. She was flattered. She was also extremely curious and this made up her mind.

"Better to know a secret you can't share than not to know one at all! So okay, you win." The voice was flippant, the smile teasing but half way through acting out the childish oath of 'cross my heart and hope to die', she saw the coldness in Russell's face and dropped her arm back. "Sorry. But I promise, I truly promise, not to talk about this when I get back. Ever, if that's what you want."

"It is." Again she was treated to a long, searching

stare.

"I mean it, Russ. I won't break your trust in me."

That finally seemed to satisfy.

"Okay." There was a long pause. "Now this may sound like some sort of fairy tale, but before you dismiss it, remember where you are sitting and how you got here...."

He related the story of the lost Kingdom and its treasure and of how he and Sam met and how they had decided that the shadow thrown by the kopje two nights before was the Black Spear pointing the way to where the treasure had been stored.

At this, Lisa's face, which had up until then been registering incredulity, turned to outrage.

"Do you mean to say you walked me half way across bloody Africa on nothing more tangible than a shadow? I could have died out there!"

Russell looked at her without even a trace of remorse on his face. "Hardly and even if it wasn't the right place, it was still as good as anywhere to head for."

Lisa pouted, barely appeased by this logical response. "So, okay, have you got any confirmation out of Dume to prove your theory that this is more than just an old African living in the middle of a great pile of rocks?" She didn't bother to hide the scepticism in her voice.

Russell answered in a calm, controlled voice, knowing that it would be difficult for an outsider to immediately accept what he knew to be the truth.

"No. He and Seki went off at first light this morning, but his spear and our amulets are the same design. See?" He undid his shirt and held out his amulet for inspection. "And look at this place. The way its protected. No ordinary African would go to all this trouble. Why should he? There's also no doubt that Dume knows about the amulets. I doubt he would have offered us sanctuary without them."

Lisa reached over and took the amulet in the palm of her hand, thumbing its delicately worked texture. It was a beautiful object. With a seductive smile she tucked the amulet back under Russell's shirt and patted his chest.

"Okay, so supposing you're right, why keep it a secret?"

"Oh, come off it, Lisa!" Russell exploded. "Can you imagine the plundering that would go on if the treasure and location were to become common knowledge?" This time it was Russell's turn not to hide his irritation.

"Black, white, or both, they'd crawl all over this place, destroying it – and its sacred history. There's nothing like fabulous wealth to corrupt. And what would the ordinary African get? A few oddments donated to a museum maybe and the rest would mysteriously disappear into untraceable Swiss bank vaults!"

"Okay! Okay! Yes, you're right. Of course you are, its just that, well, its a tall story to swallow in one go."

They sat opposite each other in silence. Lisa bowed her head, studying the ground, trying desperately to break down the story she had just been told. It was just too incredible to give credence to and yet....

She slyly looked under her lashes at Russell. His jaw was set and his eyes unblinking. He's nobody's fool, she thought and yet he believes totally in this fantasy. She conceded that the amulets had played an enormously important part in gaining her freedom and also that there was no doubting the extraordinary relationship between Sam and Russell. It was a friendship that went against all convention, so perhaps she reasoned, she should suspend rational thinking for a while and just see what occurred. She lifted her head.

"If there is treasure here, do you think Dume will let us see it?"

"We hope so. We're going to ask him when he comes back. But I think you and I present a problem to him." He smiled ruefully. "I don't think it ever crossed Dume's mind that one of the descendants of the two hundred might be white! I think he is still deciding whether to trust me or not."

"God, I hope so! It would be terrible to get this far and not be able to see the treasure, especially if Sam was allowed to do so."

"Exactly! But there's nothing we can do about it but wait and see."

CHAPTER ELEVEN

Dume and Seki finally reappeared from the far end of the amphitheatre. Russell, sitting with Lisa on the rocks by the pool, checked his watch. One o'clock. He had not seen where Dume and Seki had come from, they were just suddenly there, walking across the grass towards the cave where Dume rested several spears he was carrying against the rock. Sam clambered down from his solitary perch and joined the group by the fire as Seki helped Dume prepare a light meal of sadsza and left over meat gravy, accompanied by a mug of maize beer.

Lisa looked dubiously at the contents of her mug. Amused, Sam urged her to take a sip.

"But be careful, its quite a potent drink."

"I don't doubt it, but what exactly is in it?"

"It is just a fermented infusion of maize meal."

"It's actually a very pleasant drink," added Russell, "although afterwards it does tend to make you feel your teeth have been coated in fur. Go on, give it a go, it won't bite!"

Lisa took a sip and immediately coughed, causing smirks to appear on the men's faces. Now determined, she took another gulp and getting over her prejudice, admitted the taste was quite good.

The rest of the meal however was eaten in an uneasy silence, Russell and Sam slyly exchanging glances whilst Lisa sat impatiently in the middle waiting for one of them to start speaking. Old Dume behaved as if he was totally oblivious to the fidgeting, politely eating his meal without speaking.

Finally Lisa could stand it no longer. She gave Sam's ribs a quick, sharp dig with her elbow, causing him to give a small grunt of surprise. He turned, his intense eyes glaring their disapproval but undeterred

Lisa merely widened her eyes and made a small nodding movement towards the bowed head of Dume.

"Go on, ask him." she whispered, half in encouragement, half in command.

Sam hesitated. The moment of truth had arrived and he was afraid of disappointment but there was no-one else who could speak. At first he exchanged pleasantries with Dume but finally the burning question was asked. Was this the Valley of the Black Spear and therefore the resting place of the King's treasure?

The old man, as if unaware of how important his answer was to the rest, merely gave the briefest of nods.

With both Lisa and Russell leaning forward in desperate anticipation, Sam pressed him further.

"Would we be permitted to see the treasure, Dume?"

They held their breath and waited for what seemed an eternity as the clear, steady eyes of the African looked directly at Russell and Lisa before carefully replying.

"It's possible. Yes. The descendants of the two hundred are allowed access." There was a heart stopping moment's pause before he continued. "I have considered the matter carefully and have come to the conclusion that because of the strange but necessary circumstances that brought you here, you may all see the King's Treasure House. But..." Dume now looked severely at each of them before continuing, ".... everyone must take an oath to keep the secret. It is not yet time for the King's Royal House to be reclaimed."

Sam repeated what the old man had said and Russell and Lisa gave their solemn word. For Lisa, this promise was much easier to give than she might previously have imagined for it came to her that in fact she had absolutely no idea where she was in the first place. It would be impossible for her to lead anyone back even if she had wanted to but now, like the others, she began to see the necessity of keeping silent.

Satisfied with the assurances, Dume nodded.

"Very well, you will be allowed to see the treasure, but it can only take place tomorrow, when the sun is in the ascent."

The two men felt a thrill of anticipation surge through them, sharing the same peculiar feeling of having reached some sort of spiritual goal. A goal all the more satisfying as neither had, up until a few days before, realised they were searching for it – yet now it had become all absorbing, all important.

Lisa, who had been studying Seki as he unobtrusively cleared away the debris of the meal, excused herself and followed him. She noticed he had taken some cold fire ash down to the water's edge and with this had begun washing the plates and mugs.

"Is that where you've been this morning, Seki? Looking at the treasure?"

Seki's face lit up.

"Yes, I've been helping Dume. It's his duty to look after the treasure, to guard it and maintain it."

"Does he have help?"

"No, this is a secret place, even to the local people."

"But Dume must have dealings with the outside world?"

"Yes, he goes to the local villages sometimes, but the people never come here. They consider it a place of spirits and Dume is regarded as a witch-doctor."

Lisa, whose upbringing had given her very little contact with the African or his culture, was puzzled.

"But isn't that good? I thought witch-doctors were highly respected in your society."

"Yes, Miss, but the foot of the valley is an ancient burial ground where spirits and demons ride on the backs of hyenas during the dark hours to guard the dead. Only someone with magical powers like Dume is safe. No-one else will cross the burial ground. Dume is left alone."

Russell and Sam had been covering similar territory with Dume.

"So if the locals won't come here, what about people finding the place by accident? White men like me for instance. Have they ever come here?"

Dume clicked his tongue and shook his head.

"No." Then he recalled an almost forgotten incident.

"Once, but many years ago, white men came through the valley below the escarpment. They took with them rocks and earth as they went, but they only came as far as the river and the first waterfall. I watched them from above, but they did not venture further – they did not know the importance of this place, did not recognise the sign of the Black Spear."

Russell gave a sharp derisive laugh. "It's just as well, for if they did, they would surely have ransacked the place and left nothing to be guarded!"

As Sam translated the substance of Russell's comment, Dume frowned in disapproval, then spoke in severe tones that showed he did not think others should take the matter of his responsibilities so lightly.

"Even though I am only one, with the Spirits to give me power, I can protect this place against any who come. It took the might of a whole Nation to bring the treasure here but only one is needed to protect it. It is as secure today as it was yesterday as it will remain so tomorrow, until the Spirits tell the descendants of the two hundred that the time has come for the restoration of the Kingdom." He wagged his finger at Russell as Sam finished interpreting.

"Anyone who violates the treasure will be cursed, cursed with the same death as that which destroyed the original Kingdom. Be warned!"

Russell was alarmed that his comments had provoked and upset Dume. He had not meant to insult the old man in any way. He thought about the passage way they had squeezed through yesterday. It was impossible to move stealthily, impossible to gain surprise. One guardian could pick off attackers, one at a time, with impunity. It was an ingenious hiding place and it would take modern high explosives to blast through the rocks – the exact fate that would await it, he was sure, if the whereabouts of the treasure ever became known and resistance to its removal encountered. However Russell realised that it would be futile to take the matter further with Dume. It would only alienate the old man and perhaps make him reject the idea of letting them see the treasure. No, better to smooth over the old man's ruffled feathers and keep his pessimistic projections of the future to himself.

He quickly made amends to Dume, saying that he had not meant his comments to be taken to mean that, if attacked, Dume would fail to carry out his responsibilities successfully. It was meant more as an acknowledgement of how far, coupled with a lack of respect for the history of the black people, greed could drive white men.

Dume, pacified but still looking grave, clicked his tongue again.

"Sadly," he replied through Sam, "greed does not apply just to the white man. It is with sadness that I say that many of my own kind would also destroy the treasure house for their own gains if they could. Wealth corrupts all."

As they talked, Dume busied himself mending one of the spears he had brought back with him that morning. It once again showed intricate carvings of entwined cobras down the length of the shaft but the spear head had become loose.

Sam and Russell watched, impressed, as Dume patiently re-hammered the head into a hole he had bored in the shaft. At the same time, he had built up the heat of the fire using crude but efficient goat skin bellows which he operated with his foot. Once satisfied the charcoal was hot enough, he re-heated the coil of flat metal fitted round the shaft until it glowed red then skillfully beat it down tight again. He grunted in satisfaction as he examined the finished work.

Sam motioned to Russell and they left Dume to continue his work in peace.

"What now?"

"Dume showed me a way up to a vantage point on the crest. I thought I might take a look at the view – by myself if that's all right."

"Sure." Russell didn't mind at all. A few minutes before he had noticed Lisa climb around the first outcrop of boulders and disappear behind the rocks. He gave Sam a friendly slap on the shoulder as they parted.

"See you later then."

Sam waved his goodbye and climbed up to the top of the rocks high above the amphitheatre from where he had a superb view of the whole valley. He realised Dume had probably stood in the very same spot, carefully watching their progress as they made their way up the river the day before. He squatted down on his heels and resumed his inward look at himself. As he did so, he quietly hummed a long forgotten chant that his mother often sang as she pounded the maize. What was he to do?

He knew he could not return to the ranks of ZAPU. Something had irrevocably changed within him and made that option impossible. He felt a great overwhelming desire to see his family again. With a deep ache in his heart, he regretted the lost, empty years. Was his father still alive? What had become of his brothers and sisters? Was life for them still the same as he remembered? He began to think the unthinkable. Was there a way for him to slip back and return home? Perhaps it wasn't too late for him to resume his education, to become qualified as a lawyer, fighting for his people's rights with words, not the guns that only brought greater hatred, division and sorrow. Yet he also knew that to return home could invite retribution on his whole kraal from both sides of the conflict. What was he to do?

He stared out over the vast African landscape re-acquainting himself with his ancestral songs that gradually filled the spiritual vacuum in his soul.

Russell lost no time in finding Lisa. She was sunbathing, eyes closed.

"Hi! Mind if I join you?"

The eyes opened, the blue irises sparkling in the sun.

"No, no. Not at all."

He was treated to a wide smile as she sat herself up.

"Hey, don't get up on my account."

Lisa laughed. "Don't worry, I won't." She patted the stone beside her, inviting Russell to sit. "Where's Sam got to?"

"Oh, he's wandered off by himself somewhere. I think all this history and roots stuff has got to him."

"Well, yes, I guess it might cause more soul searching for him than for us. But.…you know more about this than I do Russ, what are you expecting to see tomorrow?"

Russell stared reflectively down at the pool below them.

"Hard to say what I really expect to find. My mind's full of the old image of treasure chests overflowing with huge diamonds, rubies and other gems, and pots of gold and silver coins. You know the sort of thing I mean, but its hard to imagine something like that exists just yards away from where we are sitting. To tell you the truth, I'm half afraid that when it comes to it, I shall be very disappointed in whatever the treasure trove reveals."

"Mmmm." Now it was Lisa's turn to quietly survey the view in front of her giving Russell the opportunity to study her striking profile. For some inexplicable reason, he felt his heart rate increase.

"Isn't this wonderful? I feel a million miles away from anywhere." The words were spoken on a long, wistful sigh. She turned her head and caught Russell's gaze. Embarrassed, Russell blurted out.

"Fancy a swim?"

"No, no. I feel too lazy. Sit down and tell me about yourself instead."

She watched in pleasure as Russell's face creased with laughter and noted that yesterday's deeply etched lines of worry had disappeared, giving his face, despite the stubble, a playful, almost boyish look.

"That's not a very original chat up line – and you a journalist! Not only that, I always thought it was the boy who was suppose to say that!"

Lisa merely gave an elegant shrug and grinned.

"Oh well, in that case I promise I'll swap reminiscences with you as we go along!"

So once again Russell found himself taken back to his childhood. He regaled Lisa with stories of his escapades, making her laugh and tut-tutt in equal measure at his pranks. The eldest by two years, he was always leading his younger brother David into trouble. Dusting out the corners of his mind, he remembered with glee the gang fights they used to engineer with their friends, using the monsoon gullies as trenches and over-ripe guavas as ammunition. The pink soft centred fruits would squash delightfully on impact, leaving the recipient covered in violent pink splodges like giant chicken pox spots. Laughing with delight, he remembered with a happy glow of nostalgia his pride and joy as a boy, the soap box his father had made them out of a set of old pram wheels and a scrounged aircraft bucket seat. It boasted a real brake and was the envy of all their friends.

He had been lucky, enjoying a happy, carefree childhood, apart from school, where the only burning memory he held was of the indignation at the almost weekly ritual of beatings he received at the hands of the missionary priests. He had little time for the Church now.

As usual, as he talked about Nairobi, Russell felt a strong pang of regret mixed with not a small amount of resentment that those days had passed for ever. Now his parents lived in a fourth floor flat in Brighton and his brother worked for an insurance company in Hove. A far cry from the lifestyle they had enjoyed in Kenya.

But it was no good dwelling on what could not be changed. He made an effort to make his conversation light, enjoying the success he was having in amusing Lisa. With this in mind, he shamefacedly confessed the scam he perpetrated against the old couple living in the house behind theirs. He would sneak into the bottom of their acre plot and collect a small selection of vegetables and then with Brad or David in tow, go round to the house and sell the vegetables back saying that he had grown them himself!

"They never twigged what I was doing and always brought the vegetables since they thought we were perfect examples of what good children should be doing with their spare time!"

"What a horrible little boy you were!"

"Oh, and I suppose you were sugar and spice and all things nice?"

"Of course. I was a model daughter. Always with my nose in a book, no trouble at all. That was until I was fifteen and discovered what boys were really for! Then my poor parents didn't know what hit them!"

Lisa's smiling face suddenly crumbled.

"What is it, Lisa? What's the matter?"

"My parents. Oh, God, Russ, they'll think I'm dead! We've got to get back and put them out of their misery." She dissolved into tears and Russell pulled her into his arms, stroking her head as she buried herself in his shirt.

Her outburst produced a sharp jab of guilt from Russell. He had not given his own parents a moments thought. Would the authorities have notified them that he was missing? He fervently hoped not. The unnecessary worry he would have caused them would be very hard to live with. His arm tightened round Lisa.

"It will be all right. One more day, then we'll be able to start making our way back and this time, we'll make it."

"Promise?" The word came out muffled as Lisa refused to lift her head from the comfort of his chest.

"Yes. We'll get across this time. I promise." Russell was glad she wasn't looking at his face as he spoke for it probably showed that he was far less confident than he tried to sound.

Lisa stayed where she was for several minutes, reluctant to break the moment of warmth but with a question still to be answered, finally pulled back, raising her tear stained face to look directly at Russell.

"And Sam? What about Sam?" She searched his face and was startled at the sudden change she found. He spoke quietly, almost menacingly.

"Sam stays this side of the Zambesi. Understand?"

Lisa's eyes momentarily widened with surprise at the implied threat in Russell's voice, but the strength of the bond between the two men had been there for her to see and then she realised, of course, Sam could not go back. To do so would mean certain death. The Authorities would never back down from the fact that he had been a terrorist. A lie would need to be told to save him and she would be expected to back Russell's story when the time came. She paused momentarily as she considered her position. Could she carry out the lie successfully? She would have to. Whatever the difference in their backgrounds, she owed Sam a great deal and she could not be responsible for leaving Russell high and dry in the dock.

"Yes. Yes, I understand completely. Of course, he'll stay this side." she reassured with a gentle smile.

Russell relaxed his grip on Lisa's arm and his eyes became soft once more. He removed a stray hair from her wet cheek and gently ran his thumb over her lips. It sent a shiver of pleasure down Lisa's spine and she moved to meet Russell's bending head but just as their lips met, an over-powering whiff of medicine had Russell sharply recoiling.

"Ugh! I'm sorry, Lisa, but that has just got to be the world's most effective turn-off. It's a real passion killer!"

Lisa gave a small, understanding sigh. "I know. I suppose I've got used to it a bit but every now and again it still catches me off guard too." She wrinkled up her nose. "I bet my Pa would have liked a bottle of this when I was young!"

The subject of her father being brought up again almost had Lisa faltering, but determined not to spoil the enjoyment of the afternoon, she purposely put the thought out of her mind and laughed.

"It would certainly have ensured I stayed in at night and did my homework!"

Russell joined in the laugh but as it died, both were aware of the mutual attraction running like an electric current between them. Russell cupped her head in his hands and pulled her to him, this time firmly planting his lips on hers. She gave way and his tongue found her warm mouth. His hands moved down towards her neck and in doing so, elicited a small cry of pain from Lisa. Russell instantly pulled back, his hands dropping down to clasp her shoulders.

"Sorry! I forgot."

Lisa took his right hand to her lips and kissed it tenderly.

"I'm the one who's sorry."

The moment gone, Russell planted a kiss on her forehead.

"One day, given the chance, I'll like to go further than that."

His reward was a heart-stopping smile as from under her lashes, she purred "Don't think I won't hold you to that." The smile broke into bubbling laughter. "Come to think of it, I bet you're a real lady killer in your uniform!"

Russell laughed with her but his mind, still caught up in his youth, flashed back to the gawky teenager clumsily attempting to chat up the girls outside the Thorn Tree coffee shop in Nairobi. They had always seemed to prefer stirring their coffee to listening to him – unless he was on his bike. Then there had been no end of girls wanting to go for a ride. In those endless, perfect, sunny days of youth, riding his Triumph motor bike on the red murram roads with the wind blowing straight onto his face had given Russell a sense of freedom that had never been equalled. He sighed.

"Me, a lady killer? On the contrary, I'm quiet, shy, inoffensive ....."

They laughed and talked, easy in each others company, until the heat of the day had passed into the cool of the evening. Everyone gathered by the fire as

Seki finished turning the spit on which fresh guinea fowl were basting but as they settled around the fire, the mosquitoes began to bite.

"I don't know what kind of berries that dye came from Sam, but I tell you, it was bloody marvellous at keeping the mozzies at bay. I don't suppose Dume has anything like that?" He finished his sentence with a sharp slap to the back of his neck.

Dume shook his head with laughter. His toughened skin had long ago become resilient to insect bites.

They ate then quickly settled down on their mats to sleep, the three inside the cave all yearning for the following day to arrive. Lisa, allowing the comfort of the kaross to envelope her into a well contented drowsiness murmured, "It feels a bit like Christmas Eve, doesn't it Russ?"

"Ha! Yes. You're right." He chuckled quietly, almost to himself. That peculiar build up of excitement and expectation that only Christmas could generate with all those intriguingly bright coloured parcels just waiting to be opened was exactly how he felt tonight. "What about you Sam? What made you go to bed all excited?"

His answer was a raucous laugh. "That is not for a lady's hearing!"

There was more laughter but as Sam drifted off to sleep, his mind returned to the thoughts that had haunted him during the past day – recollections of his home in the beautiful Matabele hills. He could clearly visualise the group of huts that had made up the kraal, hear the songs as the people gathered round to hear the stories of the past. He could even conjure up the smells of cooking and wood smoke and recall the excitement that kept him awake the night his Father had announced he was old enough to go with the other young men for his initiation into manhood. He inwardly sighed. It all seemed so very, very long ago.

As the dawn light filtered through the darkness of the cave, the three occupants awoke at the first sign of movement outside. The pent up feeling of excitement like children waking up to Christmas Day was still with them. They dressed rapidly and hurried outside in eager anticipation. Seki was lighting the camp fire and Dume was busy milking one of the goats in his usual unhurried manner.

The three tried to restrain the feeling of impatience, washing and eating breakfast as casually as they could, but the still warm milk was drunk with indecent haste.

Dume, smiling to himself, beckoned Lisa to him. He carefully examined her neck. He grunted his satisfaction as he gently applied some fresh medicine around the wound that had almost completely healed and returned to a healthy pink colour. He then looked at her feet. This time he did not bandage them with the leaves but merely rubbed the mixture directly into her skin. Incredibly, the swelling had all but reduced back to normal and Lisa felt the tears of gratitude well up. Impulsively she reached out and touched Dume's arm, breaking her normal reticence in coming into direct contact with black people.

"I... I don't know what to say other than 'thank you' for all that you have done."

Dume, not understanding the words but sensing the sentiment of what she had said, smiled broadly, showing the gaps in his teeth. He moved away, collecting from the entrance of the cave the four spears he had patiently worked on the day before. Then, with Seki at his heels, he called the others to follow him.

At last! The three lost no time in joining Dume and Seki as they crossed to the far side of the open grass area towards the solid wall of rock. Dume came to a halt in front of the largest of the boulders which projected slightly from the others.

Above, a huge, ancient fig tree grew, its massive

roots flowing down to the ground following the curve of the crevice between the large boulder and its neighbour.

Dume caught hold of one of the roots and without difficulty clambered up the boulder and stood triumphantly looking down at the amazed faces below him. He called Seki who climbed the root in an instant. Sam looked at Russell who nodded for him to go first and with Sam pulling from above and Russell lifting from below, Lisa managed to haul herself up.

When Russell arrived at the top, Dume turned towards the fig tree. In the shaded recess at the base of the immense tree where its trunk divided into two major root systems, Dume pulled away a small triangular wooden door, so skillfully concealed behind the trunk that it would be all but impossible for a stranger to detect. As the door was removed, a narrow passageway very similar to the one that had originally brought them into the centre of the rocky hideaway was revealed.

Ducking through the door, Dume beckoned everyone to follow. As they edged their way down the tunnel, they found themselves on a much wider path. Dim shafts of light filtered through from cracks in the rocks above and heightened the eerie feeling of entering another world.

It seemed to Russell that they were moving in a gentle clockwise direction. The muffled roaring that he had heard since entering the passage way grew louder as they walked and when Dume brought them to a halt, he was positive they were standing directly behind the rock wall of the waterfall.

To their left, stood a heavy boulder on which was carved two entwined cobras, identical to the design on Russell and Sam's amulets. Above them was drawn the outline of a falcon type bird perched on a chevron patterned base that Russell recognised as the

Zimbabwe Bird. It set his pulse racing and vanquished any lingering doubts that he would be disappointed in the treasure. With surprising ease Dume rolled the boulder slowly aside making Russell wonder whether it was on some form of mechanism. His interest, however, quickly moved on as an entrance to what appeared to be a deep cavern was revealed.

Torches made out of bundles of resin soaked twigs stood in a large urn by the entrance, and on a ledge in the rock, flints were ready to hand. Russell pulled out his cigarette lighter from his shirt pocket and offered it to Dume. His steady hand belied his inner state of high excitement.

Each was handed a torch, then with Dume leading, the group entered the cavern itself. Cool, fresh scented air greeted them causing the torches to flicker and dance shadows on the walls. It took a few moments before their eyes got accustomed to the unusual light but when they did so, spontaneous gasps of amazement came from Russell, Lisa and Sam.

Around the walls, three rows deep, stood racks of spears. Too many to count, they stood in their hundreds, all with wooden shafts beautifully carved with the cobra motif and polished to a deep black shine. The spear heads glinted sharply, ominously, in the glow of the torches. The walls were completely covered by cowhide shields and in the centre of the room, displayed on a table that had been painstakingly hewn out of the rock, lay many battle axes and knobkerries, their handles beautifully carved with snake designs. They looked prepared for instant use and giving free reign to his imagination, Russell visualised the awesome sight of an impi of Zulu like warriors charging out of the interior. He could hear their deep melodious chants, feel the ground beneath him vibrate to the stamping of their feet as in unison, they beat their spears against their shields. It was not just the coolness of the cave that made him shiver.

Dume spoke in a reverent whisper. Sam translated. "These are the ceremonial weapons, carried only by the King's bodyguard."

Speechless, they moved slowly down the rows of spears until they came to a heavy beaded curtain. Dume and Seki pulled the curtain away from the centre to reveal another small chamber. Each side of the entrance, glinting in the half light two massive Zimbabwe birds stood guard. On plinths and standing ten foot high, the magnificent birds stunned the visitors. Between the statues, two crossed spears with the exquisite cobra designs running down the length of the shafts blocked the passageway. Again ten feet tall. Again, tied around the neck point where the spear heads met the shafts, were the warning, long black feathers of the Widow Bird.

Russell stood open mouth, marvelling at the beautiful workmanship that had gone into creating the objects. He moved closer, hardly able to believe his eyes but touching one of the birds confirmed his thoughts.

"My god, it's all solid gold! They're absolutely fantastic!"

With mounting excitement, the three visitors were taken past the Zimbabwe Birds to face a final beaded curtain. Drawing the strings of beads aside, Dume allowed them through.

One by one they passed through into the King's chamber and stood spellbound at the sight that greeted them.

Standing centre stage on a plinth covered in animal skins – Russell could make out lion, zebra and impala – was an enormous ebony wood chair, intricately carved with two cobras, one growing from each of the front feet of the chair, their bodies coiling and twisting around the legs and arms, finally slithering up the back to meet, heads entwined, at a point above where the King would have sat. Thrown across the back and seat of the throne, lay leopard skins, the symbols of a great Chief.

Forming a natural arch behind the chair were two massive elephant tusks and in front of the plinth stood a small leather stool. On this sat a small hand coiled, ornate earthen pot in which some leaves and bark smouldered, emitting a faint heady smell, reminiscent thought Lisa of the joss sticks she and her friends used to burn at the height of their student days.

Laid out, in a fan shape from the elephant tusks to the front of the throne, were rows of more spears, axes and knobkerries, the back row full size and the front row miniature versions of the same. All of them had the same intricate design and all were made of gold.

"These," said Seki full of importance, pointing to the large spears, "are the King's own weapons. The smaller ones belong to his wives and children."

"What's that burning, Seki?"

"That, Miss, is to keep the insects and damp away."

"Well, it must work, everything is so beautifully preserved and the air so fresh."

"Dume works hard every day to keep it safe."

"Yes, I'm sure he does, Seki."

Reluctantly, they forced their eyes away from the imposing throne to explore the rest of the room.

Everywhere stood hard compressed mud plinths of differing sizes, shapes and height. On some were displayed earthenware pots full of gold bangles, chains, rings and amulets. On others, delicate porcelain bowls, plates and pitchers decorated with chinese characters. Russell studied the porcelain which he was positive was genuinely old. Somewhere in the back of his mind, he recalled that someone had once told him that the Chinese had traded down the

East Coast of Africa. It had been said that the town of Malindi owed its name to them. Was it really possible?

On other plinths stood wood carvings and bronzes depicting fertility gods, different spirits and animals. Lisa was captivated by the elaborate head rests and carved stools inlaid with designs made from strands of gold wire.

"These designs are so wonderful. It's incredible to think they were made without modern techniques."

"I know. Humbling, isn't it." Russell spoke in an awed undertone as he moved slowly around the room, aware that what he was looking at was not a white man's fantasy treasure trove of gems but more importantly, the priceless, irreplaceable relics and artifacts of a long lost but fabulously wealthy African civilisation.

He closely examined the bronzes. He was stunned. He was positive that they were Benin bronzes from the West Coast of Africa. On the walls hung ceremonial masks made of wood, ornate feathers and grasses.

"Sam, could this antelope mask come from the Bakwele Tribe?"

"The what?" It was Lisa who spoke.

"The Bakwele Tribe from the Congo. And this! These brass and copper plated figurines look as if they come from the Bakota Tribe in Gabon."

"How come you know about these tribes?"

"Oh, I studied African Art as a project at School. See, this exquisite figurine here, I'm sure that's a carving from the Makonde Tribe in what's now Southern Tanzania." It had to mean these people were trading right across Africa, just like Mukora had told him.

The variety and amount of objects was staggering. Russell, Lisa and Sam wandered slowly around the room, staring in hushed reverence at the wonderful array of treasures, finding it difficult to fully comprehend what they were seeing.

"Dume, where did all this come from?" Lisa asked. "How did it get here?"

"Come, it is time to leave. We will talk later." was all he replied.

They were overawed and reluctant to leave but Dume, politely but insistently ushered them out of the room, back through the anti-chamber and into the arsenal.

Lisa delicately stroked the glass smoothness of the shaft of one of the spears as they walked past, wondering about the men and women who had lived in that long gone Kingdom. Her mind was in a turmoil, for what she had seen had dramatically but conclusively turned upside down all that she had been taught from a girl: that the Africans were a backward and unintelligent race of people who did not know the real meaning of civilised living and therefore had to be dealt with accordingly. She doubted whether many of her compatriots would believe that such beauty and wealth could have come from a black kingdom – especially such an ancient one – and any attempt to suggest such a thing would probably be treated with utter ridicule. Yet how could she dismiss all that she had just seen? It was a sobering thought to realise just how closed all their minds were to the idea that the black man had more to offer than just servitude.

This trend of thought alarmed Lisa for it threatened to undermine her self confidence in her own race and its guiding principles. Faced with such a dilemma, she tried to block all such radical thoughts from her mind, admitting only that Russell had been right. This place was too wonderful to be discovered until people could appreciate exactly what it meant and could be trusted not to destroy or denigrate it. Until then her lips were sealed.

She was brought back from her reverie by Dume

gently taking the torch from her. She rubbed her arm, suddenly aware of how much it ached from holding the torch aloft for so long. Dume snuffed out the flame of the torches on the ground then carefully rolled the entrance stone back into place. Taking the still smouldering remains of the torches with him, he led the way back through the passage way and out into the hot, blinding dazzle of the mid-day sun.

CHAPTER TWELVE

They returned from the caves, astonished by what they had seen. Gathering back around the camp fire, they sat attentively whilst Dume, Seki by his side, spoke to them about the history of the treasure.

"Once..." he began, "... a great Kingdom existed across this land. The people were prosperous, growing rich on the trade routes that criss-crossed the country. Many different cultures met and exchanged goods, bringing wealth and diversity to the people. The land itself was lush, the hunting plentiful and the living easy. The King himself lived in a great city of stone to the south where every year the people would come to pay their taxes and renew their allegiance to their ruler."

Russell involuntarily let out a low whistle of exclamation at hearing Dume's words. Immediately the image of the Zimbabwe Ruins that lay hundreds of miles to the south by Lake Kyle in Rhodesia came to his mind. It was here that modern man had first discovered the Zimbabwe bird. Excitedly he broke in on Sam's translation.

"Wow! Sam, do you think Dume could be saying that the Zimbabwe Ruins and the King's Capital are one of the same thing?"

"Oh don't be silly, Russ," interrupted Lisa without thought. "Everyone knows that the Ruins were built by the Arabs or..." She bit her tongue, silenced by the smouldering, disdainful glare from Sam.

"You mean like a lot of your fellow whites, you do not think an African would be capable of successfully putting one stone on top of another?"

She wilted under the fierce stare and visibly winced as each word of his biting remark hit her.

"No. No! I...I didn't mean that, it .... its just...."

Russell rescued her.

"The truth is that no-one is absolutely sure who built, or lived, in the Zimbabwe Ruins. It used to be said it was Arab. Then some thought that it was possibly something to do with an eastern invasion from Persia, whilst others gave credence to influence from China. Now most believe it was built by an ancient African civilisation long since lost to the world. I've been there and seen the ruins for myself. They're fantastic. You really have to see them for yourselves to believe it. The walls are made from granite blocks as big as this." He made a wide gesture with his arms, "All hand trimmed. Its amazing to think they are still standing today despite the fact that they have no mortar binding them. Whatever the true history, there's no doubt the original City was built by skilled craftsmen and .... " He gently rubbed Lisa's chastened cheek. ".... don't ever believe, Lisa, that those people couldn't be black. They probably were."

Immensely embarrassed, Lisa feverently wished she could take back the last few minutes but more, for the first time in her life, she felt ashamed of her preconceived ideas on the natural superiority of the whites over the blacks. She brought her lowered eyes up to Sam.

"Sorry, Sam."

Seeing the genuine remorse on her face, Sam regarded Lisa a little more benignly. Perhaps with her background, it wasn't surprising she spoke out the way she had. She still had a lot to learn but at least she was trying to be more open minded. Sam drew a deep breath. "It's okay. Forget it."

Dume looked puzzled by the sudden hostility between his guests. He touched Sam's hand and inquired if all was well, wanting to relieve the uncomfortable atmosphere. Sam reassured Dume that all was well, passing on Russell's enquiry.

"Dume says he's not sure whether the ruins you are talking about are the City or just one of the major trading centres that existed. The actual location of the King's City seems to have become lost in the mists of time. All he knows is that it was situated to the South and was the greatest City of its time."

Dume patiently waited for Sam and Russell to finish their conversation before resuming his story of how the City had become too proud of its own prosperity, falling into moral decline, the people scornful of the shamans that prophesied doom if they did not change their ways. So, finally, the Spirits lost patience and cursed the people with a terrible sickness that made them go thin and die.

Dume fell silent, looking at the ground as he clicked his tongue at the folly of his ancestors. He then related to his eager listeners the story of the epic journey made by the people of the Kingdom. They were called from all corners of the land to gather at the chosen spot and labour to carve out the caves from the granite rock, whilst, led by the King himself, a formidable caravan of men, beasts and treasure left the Capital and made the long journey to this place. Many thousands died of the wasting disease but after many months, the caves were ready. It was then that the King summoned the chosen warriors to leave the protection of the isolated kraal where they had been kept safe from the ravages of the plague, to make their way to the Valley.

The great treasures were stored in the caves, the door concealed, the entrance blocked by boulders with only the narrowest of accesses chiselled out and when all was complete in a great ceremony before the assembled crowd, the King's favourite son was anointed as successor. He and the two hundred warriors were blessed by the witch doctors and given the amulets that held strong magical powers to protect against evil and to curse those that defied the King's command, after which a great sacrifice of the people took place in order to keep the whereabouts of the treasure a secret. Only the two hundred hand picked warriors were entrusted with the sacred knowledge.

When all was done, the King's son ordered a small garrison to stay and guard the treasure before leading the others away to disperse across far distant lands to await the time of restoration.

It was thought that this would happen soon but the plague ravaged the land, killing the King's household and virtually all the people, leaving the land empty and desolate. In time, strangers came and called the land their own. The few remaining people, no longer strong or mighty could not fight the newcomers and the kingdom was lost.

"To this day," Dume concluded, "we who are the guardians of the treasure await the new Kingdom that will one day arise from the ashes of the old."

"How did you come to be here, Dume?"

"I have always been here. My Father and his Father and his Father before him were all guardians of the treasure. When I was young, I took a wife and we had a son. But when he was not much older than Seki here, he was killed by a wounded lion that attacked him outside on the plain whilst he was walking back from the village. My wife mourned our son so that she did not want to live anymore. I buried them both alongside their ancestors in the valley."

Touched by his obvious sorrow, Lisa and Russell murmured their feelings of sympathy. Sam placed a comforting hand on the old man's shoulder.

After a brief pause to collect himself, Dume continued.

"I could not bear to take another wife but the Spirits assured me that when the time was right, they would send me a successor so that I could teach him all that he should know. In the past, descendants of the warriors came to pay homage. I can still recall them visiting in my youth but they became fewer and fewer. These days no-one comes. I am afraid that the young do not believe in the old ways like their fathers did. But now," he spread his arms out in an open embrace to the three adults, happiness returning to his moist eyes, "now the Spirits have made good their promise and sent me Seki."

Lisa stiffened in surprise as she heard these last words.

"Seki, is that right? You're going to stay here?"

He nodded.

"Are you sure? You know that I will look after you. I'm sure, in the circumstances, the Authorities will let me take you back to South Africa with me."

The boy vigorously shook his head in denial.

"No. Thank you, Miss Barnard but I want to stay. I want to stay with Dume."

"Well, I don't know." Lisa sucked in her lower lip. She felt in a quandary. She was not legally responsible for the boy yet she felt she had a duty to look after him following the death of his father who had, after all, been in her employ at the time. She turned to Russell for support.

"What do you think, Russ?"

Russell, still entirely engrossed in the idea of possibly knowing the true origins of the Zimbabwe Ruins, continued to play with a stick, unconsciously drawing entwined cobras in the cold ash at the fire's edge. He looked up startled when he heard his name called.

"What? Oh, well, if the boy wants to stay, why not. Its obvious he's happy here and I'm sure Dume will be like a father to him. What's he got if he comes with us? You said yourself that he has no family, that's why his Father had him with him on the trip. I'm sorry Lisa but I don't think taking him to South Africa is such a wonderful idea. It's hardly going to give him a good start in life, is it? No matter how well intentioned your actions, you can't give him equality. That's what he'll have here."

Once more Lisa was brought up sharply, stung by the strong anti-apartheid feeling amongst the others, even Russell. Trying to justify her lifestyle, she blurted out.

"I can give him a permanent roof over his head, food, even a job."

"What as?" spat Sam. "A house-boy?"

The old tension between them threatened to erupt so Lisa, feeling vulnerable, decided it was best to change tack.

"Well, what if something should happen to Dume? Who would be able to help Seki? And he'd be lonely!"

Despite the strained atmosphere, Sam laughed, amused by Lisa's last concern.

"The descendants of the warriors are not eunuchs you know and are not sworn to lead a life of solitary existence. Quite the contrary. As they are charged to keep the legend alive, Seki will undoubtedly find a wife in the next few years. Just look around you. What better place to raise a family? They are not completely cut off from the outside world. There are two villages within a day's walk."

Lisa was reluctant to concede the point. City bred she was not sure a small village six or seven hours walk away constituted sufficient social contact for the boy and there was the question of his continued education to be considered.

"The boy can read and write. What he will learn here is far more important and he will be his own man, not a second class citizen doing menial tasks." It was Sam's final word on the matter.

Lisa turned to Russell for support but he merely

shrugged. He wanted no part of the argument. Lisa pouted. Here she was trying her best for the boy and being attacked by those who should be siding with her!

A brooding silence followed so that eventually Russell felt obliged to mediate.

"Seki's nearly thirteen. I think thats old enough for him to decide for himself. We should respect his decision." He turned to Seki.

"You have the choice Seki of going with Miss Barnard to South Africa, where I am sure she will look after you to the best of her ability, or staying here with Dume to help look after the Treasure House. What do you say?"

"I wish to stay here." The boy replied without hesitation.

"You understand what that will mean?"

"Yes."

"Positive?" Seki nodded. "No doubts or questions?"

"No. I can understand what Dume wants me to do and soon I shall know his language too." He inched himself closer to Dume's side. "I wish to stay here."

"Well, that seems conclusive enough to me. The boy stays."

In the face of such overwhelming opposition, Lisa conceded defeat.

"Oh, well, if you're sure...." She let the sentence trail off unfinished. Seki stood up and gave Lisa one of his broad smiles.

"Thank you, Miss Barnard." He left the camp fire and began to prepare some food.

After eating, the men continued to talk but Lisa slipped away into the cave. She rested on her bed, feeling rejected. She turned one way then the other as she attempted to avoid facing the confusing thoughts in her head but it was no good. On her back, staring up at the blackness above her, she resolved to critically analyse her views.

The truth when she admitted it, hurt. She had always prided herself on being a liberal but now she knew she was not. It had all been a pretence, just a silly adolescent attempt at rebelling against her parents. Inside she was as racist as they were and if she needed proof, she had no need to look further than her relationship with her old ayah.

She had always protested loudly, too loudly, that she loved her devoted Louise more than anything but what she had actually done as a spoilt, over confident child was to indulge in shameful emotional blackmail. She had taken advantage of Louise, allowing Louise the privilege of doing chores and pandering to her whims in return for nothing more substantial than a careless hug. Now came the awful deflating realisation that she had never once considered Louise's feelings or needs as a person in her own right. Never treated her as an equal. She had only ever been selfishly interested in Louise as a servant. It all made uncomfortable meditation and it was a very subdued woman who finally fell asleep, vowing to be more aware of her attitude in the future.

Later, as the two men made their own way to the cave, Sam tapped Russell on the arm, indicating that he wanted to speak to him alone. They moved slightly away from the entrance.

"There has been a lot of thunder today." Deep concern was in Sam's voice.

"I know. I heard it too – and the air has become noticeably more heavy and still."

"I think it is time we got you back to the Zambesi."

There was a long pause, both men reluctant to be the one to put in motion the move that would take them away from the idyllic place of their dreams.

"You're right. Tomorrow. There's no reason to stay beyond tomorrow."

"No. I'll speak to Dume."

There was another long pause.

"Sam, do you think Dume will let us take one last look at the treasure before we go?"

CHAPTER THIRTEEN

As the sun rose to its zenith, the small group stood hesitantly on the ledge by the entrance of the cave that would take Sam, Russell and Lisa back to the outside world. Reluctant to say the final goodbye, they shuffled their feet in awkward silence.

That morning Lisa had changed back into her jeans and blouse. It had felt strange to be putting safari boots back on her feet. For her own peace of mind, she had decided that she should tackle Seki one more time about staying behind.

"Seki, you did a marvellous job mending my blouse."

"Thank you, Miss Barnard." She had knelt down in front of the boy, taking hold of his two arms, her anxious eyes searching his face.

"Are you really sure you want to stay?"

"Yes."

"Leave the boy alone, Lisa. He's made up his mind."

"But...."

"No buts. Come on, Sam and Dume are waiting for us."

At that, Seki had escaped her grip and rushed ahead whilst Russell had propelled her out of the cave. Dume and Sam had already climbed the fig tree and stood waiting, Dume patiently Sam impatiently, for Lisa and Russell to join them by the wedged door.

Knowing it to be their last opportunity, Sam, Russell and Lisa had spent the morning in the Treasure Chamber, hungrily feasting their eyes on the fantastic array of objects. Again there had been a shared sense of awed respect as they marvelled at the sheer size and beauty of the throne and its regalia.

Sam had walked slowly, silently, behind the other

two, intent on committing to memory every minute detail he saw. It was imperative to him that he remember everything correctly so that he could describe the rooms accurately when he spoke to his father, as he now believed he would. Never had he felt so proud of his blackness as he did inside the Throne Room, confronted as he was by the visual proof of his people's glorious heritage. He had felt himself stand tall. No white man would ever be his superior now simply because of the colour of his skin.

Staying until the last possible moment, loath to allow Dume and Seki to shepherd them outside, the trio had left with more than one backward glance.

Gathering their few belongings, they had accepted the gift of provisions from Dume who, after carefully packing some strips of dried buck meat and pats of cold sadsza into Sam's rucksack, had collected his spear and slowly led the subdued procession back up the narrow path to the mouth of the cave.

For the last time, he spoke. Sam turned to Russell and Lisa.

"Dume thanks us for listening to the voices of the Spirits that called us to bring Seki to him. He says Seki will grow tall and strong and be a true warrior."

Lisa bent down and hugged Seki.

"Take care of yourself." She pulled away, tears welling up in her eyes. She patted the boy's thin arms, then satisfied that she had done all she could for him, stood up. Dume held out a small leather pouch that he had been carrying with him. Smiling and nodding, he made it clear that she should accept it.

With trembling hands that suddenly seemed clumsy and out of control, she opened the bag and gasped in delight. Inside was the beautiful carved ivory comb. She carefully pulled the drawstrings of the pouch tight, slipped it around her neck and tucked the precious bundle inside her blouse. A lump rose in her throat as she tried to speak, overwhelmed by the realisation of the magnitude of the trust Dume had demonstrated by voluntarily giving her the precious memento. The right words, normally so easy to come to her, failed to form in any coherent way in her head. She gave up the struggle and merely went on tip-toe and kissed Dume on the cheek, hoping that it somehow conveyed her inner gratitude. Dume looked abashed and clapped his hands in amazement, a broad grin spreading across his face.

Raising her arms in an inadequate farewell gesture to the two that were staying behind, she abruptly turned and walked through the spears into the shadowy half light at the back of the cave, wiping away the tears with her hand as she tried to compose herself.

Sam laid an affectionate hand on the top of Seki's head.

"Look after the old man, Seki and look after yourself."

He embraced Dume, then too choked to stay longer, hurriedly joined Lisa.

Russell had stood to one side, the emotional tide rising in him as he watched the others say their sad farewells. Now it was his turn. He shook the proffered hand of Dume, clasping both his hands around the bony one of the old man. His voice broke as he spoke.

"Its been a privilege to be here. Thank you for all that you have done for us."

Dume smiled, understanding the meaning of Russell's words. He placed his spare hand over Russell's and shook them with a quick movement.

Breaking off the handshake, Russell took the amulet from around his neck. He looked at it for a long moment, seeing only a wizened old African, his white wiry hair receding and his eyes milky with age, laughing loudly as he told a small boy the story of why some men were white and some were black. Blinking to clear his vision, fearing the emotion within him would uncontrollably spill over, he quickly pressed the amulet into Seki's hand.

"This was given to me a long time ago by my friend Mukora, who, having no son of his own, entrusted it to me saying that one day I would find the right person to hand it on to. I think he would want you to have it."

Seki's fingers tightened on the amulet. He lent against Dume who put a comforting arm around the boy and nodded his approval to Russell who quickly moved to join the other two. The three turned and lifted up their arms in salute to the two figures now only dark silhouettes outlined against the bright light behind them. Dume raised his spear, the sun's rays catching the polished blade making it glint and sparkle as if it had a life of its own. He spoke in a chant. Russell didn't know what he said, but was sure he had heard it before and was sure that it was the same blessing that Mukora had bestowed upon him all those years before. Sam heard the words and as he listened, the idea that bringing Seki to Dume had been the fulfilment of his life's purpose grew within him until it became a certainty that left him with a serenity of mind that had long been missing.

Then Dume fell silent, lowered his arm and he and Seki were gone.

Neither Sam, Russell or Lisa spoke or moved for several endless minutes as they continued to stare at the now empty ledge. Loathe to turn their backs on the tranquillity they were leaving, Russell finally tore his eyes away from the sunlight and taking out his torch, began the tortuous route back to the outside world. Lisa silently followed, leaving Sam to lift his arm in an unseen last salute to the empty cavern before he too started to decend the steps back down to the tunnel, the first cave and the waterfall. As before, the heavy feeling of being trapped enveloped him as he started his journey. He began to sweat profusely and had to fight to control his breathing by concentrating on the dim shaft of torch light he was following. An agonising fifteen minutes later, Russell was pulling him to his feet and they were through the cave, over the fallen boulders and back on the ledge looking out onto the world beyond the valley.

Sam thankfully gulped in the air, the perspiration drying on his body as the feeling of space calmed his nerves. From the vantage point of the ledge above the waterfall, he joined Russell in scanning the near and far horizons. It was all deceptively peaceful, with no unusual movement to be seen over the scorched and sun baked land. Nevertheless, he could feel the renewed tension in Russell, who now spoke to him without a smile and whose eyes had become hard and wary.

It felt strange to have to worry about enemies again and the re-emergence of the seriousness of their situation began to slowly creep into each of them, making them withdraw into themselves as they made their way down to the bottom of the cliff.

"Its probably best if you go first and check everything is clear."

Sam nodded. He waded through the water and edged cautiously out of the shady glade. He was immediately struck by the unexpected fierceness of the heat that smothered him like an all embracing blanket, but nothing disturbed the heavy silence. He whistled but receiving no answer, went back to the others.

"Okay. Its clear!"

Once back out on the open plain, the three stood, eyes focused upon the distant mound of rocks. It had been decided to make for the kopje and spend the night there to bid the Valley of the Black Spear one final goodbye, but now the scale of their trek, which they had deliberately put to the back of their minds, had to be faced and it completely overwhelmed them. Each was tempted to return to the serenity of the hidden glade.

"Come on," said Sam, decisively. He slung his rifle over his shoulder and strode out towards the kopje. The other two followed.

Against all expectation, the return journey was much easier for they were both rested in spirit as well as in body and the kopje was reached by late afternoon. There had been no sightings of humans or animals on their travels but accompanying them all through the day had been low rumblings of thunder. Sam and Russell watched the ominous dark clouds massing over the distant hills with apprehension, creating an unspoken urgency in the pace they set.

Resting at the foot of the kopje, they discussed the weather.

"Look, I think we should press on until dark. We must aim to get across the river tomorrow night or it may be too late. Much as I would like to spend more time with Dume and Seki, I don't think we should contemplate the possibility of spending the next few months there. If the rain has been falling in the hills, its going to rapidly get the Zambesi into spate and when that happens, we can kiss the crossing goodbye."

"I know, Russell. I do not want you stranded this side either. Lisa, are you prepared to go on for a while longer?"

Lisa nodded her agreement. She was feeling tired but the talk of not being able to get across the Zambesi alarmed her and gave her the spur she needed to continue.

They walked on in mute single file, unable to shift the feeling of sadness and apprehension that had been with them since the morning. Finally the setting sun became a giant red orb that quickly slipped behind the western hills, plunging the plain into darkness and forcing the trio to stop.

Sinking gratefully to the ground, the weary travellers ate in silence. Lisa laid down, fidgeting on the hard earth until she curled up against Russell and slept.

The two men listened to the distant thunder as it constantly broke the night's calm with its low, angry rumbling. The moon's mellow glow that previously had offered them comfort was hidden by the oncoming storm clouds now rapidly massing across the heavens but even so, the whole landscape was frequently bathed in a ghostly white light as they were treated to spectacular shows of sheet lightning flashing across the far sky. Sometimes the thunderbolts forked down to earth with such awesome ferocity that it unsettled the animals and set off loud trumpetings of alarm from the elephants. It all re-enforced the message that the oncoming rains would not wait much longer. In the lull between lightening strikes, Sam called.

"Russell, are you asleep?"

"No." He waited, aware that Sam, unseen in the darkness was deciding whether to continue. For no apparent reason, he felt a cold sweat grip him as a deep feeling of foreboding made his stomach harden into an uncomfortable knot. Finally Sam spoke again.

"Listen. I know we agreed that I would stay this side of the river, but I have been thinking a lot these last couple of days and I want to return home." He heard the movement as Russell jerked himself upright.

"Before you say anything, let me finish. I know you can not protect me once we get across. I know the risks but I want to return to my village. As the eldest son I have a duty to my family and to the village as a whole. I want to fight the Smith regime, but I want to fight it with..." The sky was once more illuminated and for a brief second, Russell could clearly see Sam jab his head with his index finger. "....with this. To find a way through by political pressure before there is a blood bath, before everyone hates each other so much that peace and compromise are impossible."

"You think that can happen?"

Russell heard the sigh and in the darkness imagined the shrug.

"I don't know. But I want to try. Dume gave me some clothes and if I leave my fatigues and gun this side of the water, there is a chance I could slip through undetected. All I ask is that you wait until the morning before you and Lisa find help. If I walk through the night, I will be well away from you and no-one need know our connection. If I get caught, well, that will be my problem, not yours."

The knot in Russell's stomach tightened even more and he licked the sudden beads of sweat from his lips.

"It will be safer for you this side of the river."

"I know. But I want to do this, Russell."

Russell was reluctant to reply. He could not pretend he did not understand why Sam wanted to return to his homeland. In his head, he could. But his heart much preferred to leave Sam on the Zambian side of the river where his chances of survival were much better. Did he have the right to intervene with Sam's choice?

"Russell?"

He had to answer. "Okay. I'll report to the Authorities that you disappeared this side of the river. I'm sure Lisa will back me up."

They fell silent, each weighing up the possibilities that the following day might bring. Unused to the hard ground and able to gain only fitful sleep, they were happy to be on the move again before first light. As the day wore on, the heat and humidity became oppressive, an unnatural stillness pervading the landscape. Nothing seemed to move, it was if all life forms were now waiting for the inevitable deluge to begin. Dark storm clouds blocked out the sun for several minutes at a time as they sped across the sky from one horizon to the other and the thunder which had previously been content to contain itself to the distant hills, broke its confines and gathering pace as it came closer, made the lightning strikes more frequent and violent. The three hurried as fast as they could. Time seemed against them and they knew they were pitted against not only the Zambian Army but the natural elements as well.

They almost fell onto the graded earth river road. Pulling themselves back they quickly dropped down into the thick roadside vegetation, tensely holding their breath. They waited, staying absolutely still for several endless minutes but the road remained silent and empty.

"Run!"

At Sam's command, Russell rose. Crouching low, he grabbed Lisa's hand and made a dash across the road. Sam followed, his trigger finger ready as he covered their backs. They ran into thick cover then dropped to the ground. Nervously Lisa tried to steady her breathing. The pounding of her heart thumped so loudly in her chest that she imagined it could be heard in far off Lusaka. They waited, nerves taunt for several more agonisingly long minutes but still there was no movement or sound from around them. Cautiously they lifted their heads above the concealing grass. Sam spoke in a hoarse whisper.

"Going in a straight line from here, the river is about half a mile away. We have to be careful. There is a Zambian Army Post about a mile to the right of the crossing as we face it. From now on we must keep as quiet as possible and keep a look out for patrols. If all goes well, we should reach the river just before nightfall."

"Perfect timing."

"Yes – if we can do it. Okay, remember, from now on, no talking and as quiet as you can."

They recommenced their walk, Lisa tucked in between the two men who cradled their rifles in their arms, ready for instant action. Nerves were now strained to breaking point. It seemed that every twig they snapped sounded like a cannon shot in the empty silence under the oppressive sky.

With eyes and attention all focused on sweeping across the terrain ahead, his concentration singlemindedly honed for the sight or sound of other humans, Sam simply did not see the great thick patterned coils of the puff adder as it lay on the path directly in front of him.

Too late, Russell did see the snake. He caught Lisa's arm and tugged her to a standstill, hissing urgently "Sam! Sam!"

But Sam had almost walked straight into the snake which, feeling threatened, reacted defensively by recoiling back, ready to strike with its deadly venom.

Russell's warning broke the barrier of Sam's subconscious at the same time as he heard the snake's loud hiss but by then he was too close to take evasive action so stood frozen to the spot, watching in fearful fascination as the head of the snake, its mouth agape, struck.

Anticipating the snake's attack, Russell did the only thing he could think of to save his friend. He fired two shots, blowing away the head of the snake and sending shattered gobbets of flesh and blood flying into the sullen air.

"Shit!"

Russell clenched his teeth as the sound of the gun shots reverberated around the bush. They stood in silence, expecting their luck to have finally run out.

They strained to hear the tell-tale snap of a twig or see a shadowy movement in the surrounding bushes. But still nothing broke the silence. Russell looked up at the sky, now virtually painted a uniform dark, forbidding black that gave the land a gloomy light almost as if it were night.

"It might be taken for thunder."

Sam glanced dubiously at the sky above him. "Maybe." He nodded to proceed.

They skirted around the still convulsing headless body of the snake, Lisa feeling nauseous at the sight of the grotesque writhing body already covered in a black mass of flies. They could not as yet see the river, but by now they knew they were close. Very close. In their heightened state of awareness, they jumped at the unexpected and sudden sound of heavy raindrops falling with great weight onto the leaves of the surrounding vegetation.

"Lets make a run for it and just go!"

"Right, Sam, we're with you."

Russell smiled at Lisa with what he hoped passed as a look of assurance. She tried to smile back but dry mouthed with apprehension, could not. Russell took her hand and together they ran along side Sam towards the great river. As they ran, the rain changed dramatically from single drops to one continual sheet of water that rebounded from the hard earth and pelted the bodies of the three with what felt like millions of sharp stinging needles. It was if some giant sluice gate had been opened in the heavens allowing a torrent of water to pour out. Visibility was almost completely lost and the noise of the rain blocked out any other sound.

Russell gripped Lisa's hand more tightly, afraid of loosing her. They half ran, half stumbled forward, Sam along side them. Thunder now added to the chaotic sounds around them and it was only the sight of shredded leaves and bark exploding around him that made Russell realise someone from behind must be shooting at them. He shouted across to Sam but his words were drowned by the steady drumming of the rain.

He could feel Lisa faltering, dragging back his arm.

"Run! For God's sake keep running!"

They ran on but through the thunder, rain and gunfire, he still heard Sam's cry. He instantly let go of Lisa and spun round. Sam was sprawled, face down, a few feet away from him. Shaking his head to momentarily free his eyes from the rain drops streaming down his face, Russell looked searchingly into the dense blanket of rain and registered a movement to his left. Two men, dressed in camouflage were running out of the bush towards them. He forced himself to take steady aim then fired at the first man, seeing the soldier falter then crumple to the ground. As if everything was happening in slow motion, he turned his rifle towards the second man, who had knelt down to aim more carefully. Russell dived forward feeling the turbulence of the bullet's path pass over his head. Steadying himself on his elbows, he returned fire. A piercing scream carried across from the man as the hail of bullets hit his body. He was catapulted back, rifle flying into the air. Still another movement behind the trees caught Russell's eye. A third man had turned and was running away. Russell aimed, fired, but the bullets missed and the man continued to dodge and jink out of sight.

All seemed to go quiet, even the rain eased down to a steady downpour.

Russell crossed to where Lisa was kneeling helplessly besides the body of Sam. A blood stain showed on his back. Russell gently rolled him over. He was still conscious but the bullet had entered into his chest and although the hole in his back looked small, Russell knew that the bullet would have tumbled in Sam's chest causing huge tissue damage. Blood was spreading over his shirt and a thin trickle was oozing out of the side of his mouth.

Sam jerked his head towards a nearby tree trunk and Russell dragged him over to it, carefully propping him against it. Sam grabbed Russell's wrist and spoke through tortured gasps.

"Gun!"

Russell retrieved the AK from where it had been flung on impact of the bullet hitting Sam. He rested it against Sam who was desperately fumbling with his ammunition pouches.

"Ammo"

Russell knelt down and unhooked the shaking hand from the pouch.

"Here." He took out two magazines and placed them in Sam's lap then checked the one in the rifle. Sam, his face tinged with grey, tried to smile.

"Can't cheat death, three times Russell. Cheated it once with you, once with the puff adder, but not a third time."

Russell bowed his head, not knowing what to say. Just as with Bob Martin, they both knew there was nothing to be done.

With a great effort that sapped his ebbing strength, Sam struggled to remove the amulet from around his neck.

"Take it." The words were rasped out with great effort.

"I'll get it back to your Father, I promise Sam."

"No! You keep it." He paused, gulping for air, his breath rattling in his throat. "I want you to have it."

Russell nodded his still bowed head, not trusting himself to speak. He had known Sam for just ten short days but in that time they had shared so much it had seemed a lifetime, a lifetime that had forged a bond stronger than blood or colour. The agony of watching his friend die was almost too much.

"You must go. Take Lisa and go."

"I can't just leave you here."

"Go, Russell. There is no time to wait." Talking was visibly weakening Sam, who now lay in a pool of his own blood. He tightened his grip around Russell's wrist and with the greatest of effort spoke in short gasps.

"Go straight into the river..... Let the current take you. There is a bend.....a little further down stream....the current sweeps you round......takes you close to the other side. You must....you must make sure.....as you round the bend that....you free yourself from the current. If not .... Are you listening to me, Russell?"

The still bowed head nodded. "Yes, yes, I hear you, Sam."

"Okay. Now go. There is little time. They will be back."

Russell was still reluctant to move. His mind was frantic to find a way of rescuing Sam, but he knew that to move him again would only cause additional pain and hasten his death.

Sam turned his head slightly to look towards Lisa, now standing sodden and visibly shaking a few feet away, pathetically clutching the food bag to her as she waited. Tears were flowing unchecked down her face but her tongue constantly licked her lips as her eyes, wide with fear, nervously scanned the blurred darkness of the trees surrounding them. Her face registered the desperate emotional see-saw raging inside her, torn as she was between her feelings for Sam and blind panic to get away.

Sam coughed up more blood and closed his eyes. He felt immensely tired and wanted only to sleep. He was too befuddled now to work it out clearly but he knew he had paid his family's debt to his ancestors and was content that in the after life he could face them with honour. It was enough. A warm darkness enfolded him. He was not afraid. But he could still smell fear around him, could still feel his friend's anguished eyes upon him, could still register Russell's movement next to him, calling his name urgently. Reluctantly, Sam remembered there was still something he had to do before he could sleep in peace. With tremendous willpower, he re-opened his eyes and reached out a hand to Russell.

"Only you can save Lisa. Go Russell! " The last two words were barely audible. Russell pressed Sam's hand into his own and squeezed it. Their eyes met and held for a second.

"Go my friend and may the Spirits of the Ancestors continue to be with you."

"And with you too, Sam." Russell stood up, catching a deep gulp of rain and air.

Sam watched as Russell picked up his own rifle, grabbed Lisa's hand and started the run towards the river. He heard them crash through the vegetation, any pretence of caution gone. He coughed, blood spurting out of his mouth, then with fingers shaking with weakness, he held his rifle ready and waited.

Lisa almost fell to the ground at the momentum of Russell's strength pulling her forward. She had still been looking towards Sam as Russell had grabbed her and yanked her to a run.

"Don't look back!"

As they ran, lungs bursting from the exertion and terror, Russell counted.

'One, two, three,' He reached forty five by the time the first burst of gun fire was heard.

There was no time to question whether it was a one way battle. They burst through the last of the riverine bushes, tumbling head first down the bank and crashing some ten feet into the fast flowing brown river.

Picking themselves up, they waded through the water which at first was only calf deep. They appeared to be crossing a large sand bank, but then, without warning, the ground gave way underneath them, the strong current forcing their feet from under them, sweeping them away. The sheer power of the river was awesome and Russell instinctively tightened his hold around Lisa's waist as they struggled against the current, trying to keep their heads above water.

They were being swept along at such an alarming rate that Russell feared he would not get his bearings before they reached the bend. As Sam had predicted, the current itself moved them towards the Rhodesian bank. Russell could taste the panic that rose within him and tried to swallow it down as the bend came into view and they were still unable to release themselves from the grip of the current that held them fast.

Lisa had become a dead weight and it took all the reserve of strength he had to push her and himself towards the now rapidly approaching bank. Another few yards and they would be swept past the bend. His rifle, dragging at his shoulder, knocked painfully into his body as the current caught it. He let it go as Lisa had let the food bag go the moment she had felt herself being swept away. The almost overwhelming sensation of tiredness Russell felt made it seem all too easy to give up the unequal struggle and let the flow take over. Then a spindly root of a tree that had become exposed by the erosion of the bank came into his view and revived his determination. In a desperate lunge he grabbed it and to his utter astonishment, it held and checked their head long rush down stream. With strength he didn't know he possessed, Russell finally broke free of the current and pulled himself out of the water, dragging Lisa's sagging body behind him. Then began a desperate endeavour to claw his way up the high, almost sheer river bank.

Never had a bank seemed so steep or slippery to him. With nothing to grip and the earth continually falling away under his feet, he repeatedly slipped back, crashing down on top of Lisa who could do nothing but cry out in pain. The fear of being shot at from across the river spurred him on and finally he hauled himself and Lisa over the top. Too exhausted to stand, they crawled away into the relative safety of the thick bush and collapsed on the ground, spluttering and gasping for breath. It was Lisa who found her voice first.

"Are we....." she gulped agonisingly, her lungs desperate to draw more air, ".....are we in Rhodesia?" In her present state of mind, it would not have surprised her to be told that the river had played a cruel trick on them and kept them on the wrong side.

Russell shook his dripping head.

"Yes. Yes, we've made it."

In their dishevelled, broken state, the words failed to have the impact they deserved. The two curled themselves up into balls, pulling their legs tightly to their bodies, hugging their knees with their arms, the immense relief in being alive making them feel weak and light-headed. Lisa's tears mingled with the rain but Russell looked towards the far bank and wished he had the power to change the last half an hour of their lives. If he could, Sam would still be alive.

CHAPTER FOURTEEN

Russell was dimly aware of a continuing sound of sporadic bursts of gunfire from across the river. It lasted for some time but finally only the sound of the rain beat in his brain. In the gathering darkness, he stirred himself out of his stupor and with a weariness that made even talking an effort, turned to Lisa.

"Come on, we'd better move inland a way – just in case."

Lisa nodded. An air of unreality surrounded her and she found it difficult to motivate herself off the ground. Russell pulled her up on her feet and together they stumbled inland, trying to put as much distance as they could between themselves and the crossing place in the short time left before the light totally deserted them.

Russell located a suitable thicket of bushes to act as cover, lethargically deciding it was as good a place as anywhere to stop for the night. He wedged himself between two small trees and allowed Lisa to curl up beside him. He put his arms tightly around her, brushing the top of her wet head with his lips. Neither spoke but huddled in silent misery – cold, wet and hungry – waiting for the daylight.

As the hours slowly ticked by, the rain promised to ease but the thunder continued to rumble incessantly around them, creating in the darkness an atmosphere of foreboding that suited Russell's own brooding about Sam. Had Sam's body been taken away by the Zambians? Did it still lay where he could picture it, propped against the tree? The tree was less than a mile away but for all that he could help Sam, it might just as well have been in another universe. Tormented by his thoughts, Russell stared, unseeing, into the night, wincing defensively against the brilliance of each blinding lightning bolt that arched across the heavens above him. Nothing could distract his thoughts away from Sam, not even his overwhelming tiredness that made his body crave for sleep.

Would they give Sam a decent burial or leave his body for scavenging hyenas to rip apart? Russell shivered with revulsion at the very idea. Anger welled up causing a surge of heat through his body, anger directed at some unknown force that had taken his friend's life when they were so close to making it home. It seemed so unfair. So unnecessary.

'Shit, Sam. Shit, shit, shit!' His head ached as if a hammer was methodically striking at his temples and the heavy rain once more started to sluice down, re-soaking him within seconds.

With fingers that ached, even to undo the button of his shirt pocket, Russell took out Sam's amulet. Fingering it, he slowly placed the leather throng around his neck, peeling his sodden shirt from his body as he tucked it carefully inside. He could no longer hold back the emotions of pain and disappointment and for once, he was glad of the rain to help disguise his tears. He hung his head and closed his eyes in despair.

Sometime just before dawn, the rain stopped but it did nothing to make the waiting more comfortable. At the first sign of the darkness giving way to the false dawn, Russell stood up. He felt chilled to the bone and stiff, wanting only to feel the warmth of the sun on his back.

Lisa struggled to her feet. Her head pounded with tiredness and contrary to the elation she thought she would feel at being safely back on the Rhodesian side of the river, she felt strangely deflated, as if a heavy depression had descended upon her. She morosely surveyed her surroundings. How she had come to hate the bush!

"So, where do we go from here, Russ?"

"Dunno." The voice was flat, disinterested, causing Lisa to peer sharply at her rescuer. He looked gaunt and it alarmed her to see such deadness in his eyes. At once she was more aware of his deep misery than her own and her heart went out to him. Hesitantly, she touched his arm.

"I'm sorry about Sam..." She caught the fleeting wince of pain that flashed across his face at the mention of Sam's name. "...But there's nothing to be gained by dwelling on it."

Acutely aware of Lisa's need for him to take charge of the situation, if only because he could hear Sam telling him he was the only one who could save her, Russell made a supreme effort to snap out of his apathy. They were still a long way from home and he had heard of men dying out in the bush when only yards from the safety of a main road. He straightened his shoulders.

"We'll keep heading straight inland and pick up the river road. That should take us back to one of the Slope – sorry – South African bases. Here." He offered his hand and Lisa took it, thankful to see a spark of the old Russell return. Together they started on the final walk. Briefly, the sun broke through, offering promise of warmth but the tenebrous clouds forming into a blanket across the sky quickly obliterated it and brought down more ferocious rain.

Lisa looked up at the brooding sky, the rain instantly chilling her to the bone.

"I guess we made it across just in time."

"Yeah." Despite his resolve to be positive, Russell had no appetite for talk and certainly did not want to think about how close they had come to being unable to cross the river. They had Sam to thank for their freedom. Without his knowledge of the second crossing, they would never have made it back. At the memory of Sam, the heavy weight of sadness descend upon him again. He set his face hard against the weather and tried to sublimate his misery by concentrating on where he was walking. He needed to, for the ground was now saturated, the hitherto light dusty soil changing into a slippery, tacky substance that clung to their shoes, making it difficult to walk. Still, within half an hour of starting out, they reached the river road, now a wide expanse of glutinous mud, patterned with deep vehicle ruts and skid marks.

Russell looked up and down, trying to locate familiar land marks but the curtain of rain made visibility so poor, he could not detect any special features that would help him decide their exact position. Even so, it was with a certain amount of relief that he spoke.

"Well, here we are, home ground. This road takes us back either to the camp at Mana Pools or Chewore. I'm not a hundred percent sure which one is closer but I figure we're probably about mid-point between the two. Which way do you want to go, left or right?"

He watched Lisa's face, the first shadow of a smile appearing on his gaunt features as he noted her habit of pushing her hand several times through her hair whenever she was undecided, a habit he found endearing in one so normally possessed with outward confidence.

Unaware of this observation, Lisa tried to make up her mind. It felt a lifetime since she had made a decision for herself and now faced with such a simple one, she found she couldn't.

"You say."

Russell's smile broadened.

"Okay. Let's turn right. But don't blame me if I'm wrong and we have to walk all the way to Chirundu."

The armoured bucket on wheels that was the latest in mine proof vehicles was nearly upon them before they heard the engine under the din of the rain and the zombie like trance they had both fallen into as they walked.

The green vehicle overtook them then pulled up in front, a head appearing over the top. It wore a South African Police cap.

"Hey, you! What are you doing here? We haven't passed any other car on the road. Where have you come from?"

The young man's face, eyes screwed tight against the rain, was clearly suspicious at the sudden appearance of two such bedraggled creatures. It was obvious he was nervous in case they were some kind of planted decoy for a dangerous, desperate gang lurking in the nearby cover just waiting to ambush unsuspecting travellers.

Russell noted the tip of a gun barrel resting on the door frame as they approached the rear of the vehicle. He very carefully held up his hands and nodded towards the bush.

"Out there. My name is Patrol Officer Forester and this is Lisa Barnard, the kidnapped TV reporter."

"Thats right. This man has rescued me from a terrorist gang." Lisa spoke from behind the protection of Russell's shoulder.

They could see the anxiety change to utter astonishment.

"Is that so? Hey, Kurt, this guy says he's a Police Officer and .."

"Yah, yah, I heard. Just get them into the truck. Quick."

Both Lisa and Russell were bundled into the back of the vehicle which, with tyres whining and spinning in the mud as the driver gunned his engine, pulled quickly away from the pick up point.

"I'm surprised you guys are travelling this road in the rains."

"Yah, sure. You're lucky if you are who you say you are, because over the last two days, the state of the road has become so treacherous I doubt whether anyone else will try after this."

The front passenger picked up the vehicle's radio microphone and called up his base.

"We have picked up two whites. One male, one female. They claim to be missing Patrol Officer Forester of the BSAP and the TV reporter recently abducted by terrorists. Over."

There was a long pause before the base radio acknowledged their message. Russell could imagine the buzz that had gone round the base at receiving the unexpected message.

"Well, you'd better bring them in."

The rain eased off as the vehicle skidded and slid along the road, enabling Russell to recognise the terrain. He nudged Lisa.

"In case you haven't recognised the call sign, we're heading for Mana Pools."

"Yah! Almost there now." added the driver. "Then we can get you into some dry clothes."

As they approached the South African Police Base the road ran into an open area of ground that formed the defensive fire zone for the fort, itself a low structure set under trees. It was protected by a ring of barbed wire entanglement and booby traps and had a double skin wall of corrugated iron filled with soil topped off with sandbags, lashed together with metal posts. The four corners of the outer perimeter wall held machine gun emplacements but the accommodation within the fort itself was no more elaborate than a neat number of open sided green tents.

The vehicle, waved through by the guards at the gate, drove past a group of curious onlookers and pulled up sharply in front of a Lieutenant standing stiffly in its path.

Russell and Lisa's rescuers got out of the car and saluted. The Lieutenant waved them to bring out the passengers.

Russell climbed out first then helped Lisa. She immediately stepped forward, hand extended and a smile on her face.

"Do I have the pleasure of addressing Lieutenant Van Rensburg?"

The man nodded dumbly, wrong footed by such an unexpected direct approach. Lisa continued to take charge, pressing home her advantage.

"I'm Lisa Barnard. I was on my way to you after visiting the Kariba base, when we got attacked."

"Yes, that's right. But, by God, we thought you were dead!"

"I probably would have been if not for the bravery of Patrol Officer Forester here."

The Lieutenant took the offered hand, becoming more affable.

"Struth, man, your Station will go ape when they hear you're okay. They searched everywhere for you. Here, you'd better come with me and we can radio them straight away. Sergeant DeKok, take Miss Barnard to the Mess and see that she gets clean clothes. Sorry Ma'am but we've only got mens gear here but I'm sure we can find you something dry. See she gets everything she needs, Sergeant."

Before either could speak again, Lisa was briskly ushered away. Twisting round from the arm that was propelling her forward, she managed to call out 'see you in the mess tent, I'll buy you that beer' before Russell himself was led off in the opposite direction towards the communications tent. As they walked across the open square of the Fort, a helicopter parked on the pad caught Russell's eye.

"More visitors?"

"Yah, you're not wrong there. It belongs to our Brigadier. He's in the Mess tent right now, talking to one of the game wardens. He's been on a visit down here and will be flying back to Salisbury within the next half an hour. Lucky really. He'll be able to take Miss Barnard back with him."

Russell felt a sinking feeling in the pit of his stomach at these words. He had not thought about the time when Lisa would not be with him and the realisation that this was about to happen caused the blood to drain from his face.

"Are you okay, man? You look washed out."

"Yeah, sure. I'm fine. I think its just hitting me that I'm back in the land of civilisation."

Lieutenant Van Rensburg laughed and slapped him on the back as they entered the radio tent.

"Sure. I guess it will seem a little strange for a while. Here, let's call up your base then we can get you into dry clothes. Bet you could do with a beer, too."

Russell gave a tight lipped nod in response, thankful that the Lieutenant and his radio operator's attention had turned to raising Chirundu. In a better frame of mind, he might have acknowledged Sergeant Madudzi's prompt response and inwardly smiled at the ensuing incoherent conversation between him and the South Africans. It took several exasperated efforts to explain to Madudzi that Patrol Officer Forrester was at Mana Pools, alive and well. Finally Van Rensburg lost his patience and merely yelled down the microphone to be put through to the most senior Officer on duty. The airwaves appeared to go dead.

"Struth! What kind of idiot have you got operating your radio? He's really thick. We'd never tolerate a kaffir like that!"

The Lieutenant's remarks inflamed Russell. Such arrogance sat ill with him, today of all days. His jaw line tightened as he attempted to surpress his angry retort and to avoid eye contact, made a careful study of his feet. He looked up sharply however as the clear clipped voice of John Makesmith came on the air.

"Do I understand that you have Patrol Officer Forester with you?"

"Yes, that's right Sir."

"I'd like to speak to him, please."

Van Rensburg, enjoying the look of dread on Russell's face, grinned broadly as he handed the radio microphone over.

"Hey man, I think you are for the high jump!"

Russell took the radio mike with sinking heart. Hearing his Member in Charge's request brought home to him as never before just how awkward his situation was. Lisa and he had agreed the same story and he was sure she would keep to it, but explaining how and why he had gone A.W.O.L. to the satisfaction of his Superiors suddenly seemed much less certain than it had a few hours before.

He acknowledged the call, his heart beat racing. Makesmith kept the call short and sharp.

"Forester, a vehicle is on the way for you. It should be there within the next three hours. In the meantime say nothing. Understood?"

"Yes, Sir."

"We'll speak when you get back. Now hand me back to the Lieutenant."

The Lieutenant and Makesmith continued to speak but Russell's concentration in trying to follow the gist of the conversation was broken as he recognised the whine of a helicopter's rotors starting up.

He mumbled 'excuse me' to a startled radio operator and Van Rensburg as he tore out of the tent into the open square just in time to see the brigadier's helicopter lift off the ground. He saw the small face of Lisa anxiously peering out of the rear window as she scanned the ground below. As she caught sight of

Russell, the frown disappeared and was replaced by a relieved smile. She had just enough time to wave her hand before the helicopter banked over the trees and scudded away, disappearing quickly into the distance. Russell stood rooted to the ground, oblivious to his surroundings, intent only on watching the helicopter as it shrank to a dot on the horizon. The dust and noise abated and he visibly jumped as a hand came down on his shoulder.

"Just think, the lucky bitch will be home in the Republic by tomorrow. Wish it was me. Oh well, I guess there's no point in mooning. Hey, come on man, I'll take you to the Mess. You can clean up and have a beer whilst you wait for your transport to arrive."

The Lieutenant led the way, unaware of the devastating sense of emptiness Russell felt as all that had become important to him fell away. First Sam, now Lisa. He felt totally alone and bereft, numbed by the fact that his entire world had just shattered.

He stood in the shower, cleaning himself with hot water for the first time in nearly two weeks. It was a luxury that should have made him feel better, but it did not. Van Rensburg appeared, holding a razor.

"Hey, Forester, I suggest you use this. It might help when you have to face the firing squad!" He smirked, enjoying the thought of someone else getting a roasting from his superiors. "There's clean clothes out here for you, too."

Russell in sufferance, accepted the razor. He looked into the mirror and saw a stranger. A stranger with blood shot eyes sunken into black rings that melted into a spread of dark hair down his neck to the line of his collar. He began to shave away the beard and with each sweep of the razor across his face, it was as if he were stripping away all the incredible happenings of the past few days. He blinked as the familiar clean faced P/O Forester started to reappear in front of him again.

Refreshed and in dry clothes, he sauntered across to the Mess and was given a large plate of steak and eggs, which despite the lack of food over the previous twenty four hours, he found difficult to swallow. The longed for cold beer was handed to him, but it felt curiously flat and disappointing. The off duty South Africans, frustrated at having Lisa whisked away before they could question her, tried badgering Russell to tell them about where he had been and what had actually occurred across the Zambesi, but finding their questions stone walled, they grudgingly gave up and one by one left, leaving him alone. He was glad when he was informed that his station landrover had arrived to take him back.

His black mood lifted slightly when he caught sight of Alistair resting casually against the Landrover. Grinning at each other, they shook hands enthusiastically and slapped each other on the back.

"Hey man, its good to see you. We thought you were dead for sure. We searched for three days and found nothing but your gear. Where the hell have you been?"

"Come on, lets get out of here and I'll tell you on the way."

"Suits me fine. Where's your kit?"

Russell went back to the mess and collected the bag containing his clothes and webbing. Strolling over to the Communication Tent, he took his leave of his South African hosts.

As he placed the small bag in the back of the Landrover, Alistair cocked an eyebrow in his direction.

"No rifle? Bloody hell, Russ, you haven't lost your FN!"

Russell said nothing as he clambered into the front passenger seat.

"Hell, man, you're really in the shit now!"

"So everyone keeps telling me." came the dry response.

"Well, rather you than me facing the old man." Alistair's face broke into a wide, gleeful grin. "Do you realise just how many forms you'll have to fill in to get a replacement ....?"

They drove out of the South African base, giving the guards a final wave of their hands out of the Landrover windows and turned towards the lone hill at Chirundu, driving fast over the slippery mud road.

During the journey, Alistair filled Russell in on what had been happening during his absence. He started by describing the running battle between the gang of terrorists and themselves after Russell had so abruptly left the scene. The contact had gone on for several hours over a long distance resulting in six terrorists being killed and two South Africans being badly wounded and having to be casevaced out by chopper. It was the length of the operation that had made searching for Russell so difficult for no-one had seen him after they had crossed the stream and a vast area had to be covered. Finding no trace of him the first time had made the authorities reluctant to call off the search and Makesmith had ordered a second full sweep to be carried out before conceding defeat. He was now, Alistair informed Russell with no small amount of mirth, furious that his time and effort had proved to have been so unnecessary.

Russell listened first with interest then with increasing discomfort. To his growing shame he had never contemplated the effect on others that his absence would create. He had only seen his actions from his own point of view. The realisation of the turmoil his recklessness had created made him shrink into his seat and retreat into his own thoughts. Alistair finding Russell reluctant to talk beyond a few basic facts, shrugged. He guessed Russell had been told not to say anything and that was okay.

They arrived at the Station just before six o'clock in the evening. The Station Sergeant, a broad beam across his face, greeted them with a salute as the Landrover pulled up by the Station Office and came to a halt.

"Pleased to see you, Sah! The Member in Charge requests your immediate presence!"

"I bet he does!" muttered Alistair helpfully as Russell jumped out of the car and collected his bag.

His Batman, standing next to the Sergeant, eagerly stepped forward and took the kit, repeatedly exclaiming to Russell.

"Wundaful! Wundaful!"

"Thanks, Charlie. Its good to see you too. I'll be along in a moment." He turned to Alistair "Thanks for the ride. See you in the Mess for Dinner – I hope!" He banged the side of the jeep with the flat of his hand as it moved off.

"Yeah. Good Luck!"

Russell tried to tidy himself up, pulling his borrowed shirt straight and running a hand through his short cropped hair, before placing himself in John Makesmith's open doorway. He knocked.

"Come in Forester and close the door!"

Russell walked in and stood to attention. Makesmith was standing at his desk, sorting through some papers and spoke without looking up.

"Well I see you have returned to us in one piece."

"Yes, Sir."

"Hmm." There was a long pause. "As you might have anticipated, Salisbury is sending up a Special Branch Officer tonight and he'll want to see you first thing tomorrow. I hope you have something useful for him."

"Yes, Sir, I think I have."

Makesmith finally looked up. This time the young pup had gone too far. Endangering life, even one's own outside the direct and specific calls of duty was unjustifiable and in the straightened circumstances the Rhodesian forces were in, causing others extra work and wasting valuable resources was intolerable. The eyes that looked over at Russell were therefore cold and unblinking and Russell felt the first hot flush of nerves go through him.

"All right." He motioned for Russell to sit. "You'd better give me a quick run down of what's been going on."

Russell began his rehearsed story. He explained how he had become separated from the main force when chasing one of the terrorists.

"He was going to kill me, Sir, when his gun appeared to .... err .... jam."

"Damn lucky for you."

"Yes, Sir." Russell ignored the cynical overtone of his boss's interruption.

"Anyway, he made a run for it back towards the river and I took off after him. When I caught him, he wanted to make a deal."

"A terrorist suggesting a deal? I must remember that one."

"Yes, Sir." Russell coughed uneasily, keen to move on. "Anyway, he mentioned he had seen the gang holding the hostages. Apparently they had run into each other just this side of the Zambesi crossing point. He said that the gang were a different group to theirs, part of ZANLA, so if I let him go, he would take me to their camp, approximately a day's march into Zambia."

"I've heard of some stupid excuses for absences in my time ..." Makesmith's face was a mask of stone.

Russell shuffled in his seat, uncomfortably aware that this was the weak link in his defence.

"Well, yes, Sir," he hurried on, "looking back, it was of course an incredibly idiotic, not to say, risky proposition, but, well, all I can say is that at the time it all somehow seemed plausible. I can't explain it sensibly now, Sir, I realise that, but all I could think of was that there were three hostages with a – albeit – slim chance of survival and I had the opportunity to do something about it. I wasn't in a position to radio in, it was already late and getting dark and I had no idea where the South Africans and P/O Briggs had got to. There was no time to find them. I had to make a decision there and then...," Russell took a deep breath, his fingers mentally crossed "...and so I decided to go. The possibility of rescuing three of ours seemed worth the probability of losing one of theirs, Sir."

"Did it indeed?" There was no mistaking the sour note in Makesmith's voice. "Well, I hope the Officer Commanding Mashonaland, the Commissioner and all the other interested parties agree with you. You're damn lucky Forester, that you managed to bring the woman back. It's probably saved your hide."

"Yes, Sir, I'm aware of that."

"Go on!"

Russell briefly outlined the trek to the camp, giving details of two large groups they had witnessed moving towards the Zambesi. He described the raid on the camp, the death of Bob Martin and explained Seki's absence by saying that Lisa Barnard had told them the porters had taken him away with them when they had left the camp. Finally he explained their attempts to recross the Zambesi which had been thwarted by the Zambian Army going on full alert.

For the first time in the interview, John Makesmith gave a thin lipped smile.

"Yes, we wondered what had made the Zambians so twitchy. Our clandestine South African eavesdroppers picked up a lot of radio activity from the other side. I might have known it would have something to do with you."

"Yes, Sir, sorry about that. It occurred to me that Victor Troop might be puzzled at the misinformed data they were suddenly receiving. Anyway, given our situation, the only thing we could do was to head inland, keep our heads down and wait for the emergency to die down."

"And this terrorist – what's his name? Comrade Max?"

"Yes, Sir. That was the name he gave me."

"Highly unlikely to be his real name."

"Yes, Sir."

"Anyway, you say he stayed with you?" There was more than just a hint of disbelief in Makesmith's question.

"Yes, Sir. He stayed with us right to the end."

"Then what?"

"After three days, we returned to the Zambesi. It all seemed quiet and we decided to attempt a crossing. As we made to go across, we were discovered by the Zambians who attacked us. In the ensuing fire fight Max was killed."

"Bloody convenient." The sour note had returned.

Russell inwardly winced in anguish.

"Yes, Sir, but true nevertheless. The rest, I think you know."

Makesmith put down the pencil he had been twirling in his fingers all the time he had been listening to Russell's report. His face had hardly altered throughout the interview and Russell could not decide what his Superior's reaction to his story would be. When it came, it was non-committal.

"Well, put it all down on paper. I want a report on my desk by eleven sharp tomorrow morning." He nodded a curt dismissal.

Russell turned and walked out. There was no point in trying to figure out what the future was going to hold for him. If he had to face a court martial and be drummed out of the force in disgrace, it was too late to alter what had gone before. He knew without a shadow of a doubt, he did not regret going with Sam. He sighed as he flicked through the papers lying on his desk top. It was still hard to return to the mundane. He took a wad of official forms and left.

Russell made his way up to the Mess on top of the hill. As he walked into the Mess Bar, the occupants – Alistair and two other Patrol Officers – immediately slipped back their chairs and stood to attention.

"All rise to welcome back the station idiot! The beers are on P/O Forester, Nelson."

The barman grinned and served up the ice cold beers which everyone downed in one. Russell nodded for a refill. All were curious to know the details of his escapade but Russell side stepped the issue – he did not yet feel ready to laugh and joke about his exploits – by saying that until he had spoken to the Special Branch, he was ordered not to say anything. Instead, he went through to the dining room to eat a solitary meal before retreating to his room.

Alone at last, he rested on his bed, listening to the rain drumming noisily on the corrugated asbestos roof overhead. He lit a cigarette and smirked at himself. How strange it was that he had not smoked or even wanted a cigarette all the time he was in Zambia and now, back 'home', safe and in one piece, he had smoked a packet of twenty in less than ten hours.

The future haunted him with the same unanswerable questions running round and round in his head. What was his future? He had six months left of his 3-year contract. If allowed, he would honour it to the best of his ability. But what then? With a heavy heart he allowed the answer to at last solidify in his head. He had to accept Africa was not his. Accept it and not look back. Perhaps he should try his luck in Australia or Canada. After all his Grandfather had been a Mountie. Maybe that was where he should go.

His own problems settled for the moment, his thoughts returned to Sam. Guilt resurfaced. Why did it have to be Sam that died and not him? He could feel the weight of the amulet on his chest. It seemed to him that it was telling him he should no longer wear it.

He considered the position and was unhappy at the idea that Sam's life would not be honoured. To deny Sam's existence to the Authorities was one thing but to do so to his family was another. Sam's father should know what had become of his son. He should know his son had helped keep alive the guardianship of the treasure and that despite the many obstacles, had kept faith with the sacred oath.

Russell made a vow to himself. At the first available opportunity, he would seek out Sam's family and return the amulet to its rightful inheritors.

For himself, he had, however unwittingly at first, played his own part and done what Mukora had asked. Now like his life in Africa, it was over. He was finished with the Valley of the Black Spear.

He closed his eyes and slept.

CHAPTER FIFTEEN

Immaculately dressed in grey shirt, shorts and leather leggings buffed up by his batman to a shine that reflected his face, Russell stood outside John Makesmith's door at precisely eleven o'clock. He hesitated, curbing the knot of apprehension in the pit of his stomach. He took a deep breath to help regulate his breathing then knocked.

"Come!"

He opened the door and entered. Makesmith, again standing authoratively behind his desk, nodded towards the two men sitting opposite him, one of whom was a familiar face to Russell.

The large imposing Englishman, dressed coolly in a pale blue safari suit, stood up as Russell crossed the room and extended his hand.

"Russell, its good to see you again."

"Andy." Russell shook hands warmly with the Station's permanent Special Branch Officer who then introduced the stranger.

"This is my colleague, DI Roger Wood, from Salisbury."

The second man nodded and smiled. "Morning, Forester."

"Sir!"

"All right, gentlemen, I suggest we get down to business without further delay. Your report, Forester." Makesmith took the offered sheaf of papers from Russell, giving them a cursory glance through before handing the carbon copies to the two plain clothes policemen. He sat down, motioning Russell to sit on the only other spare seat, which was to one side and facing both the desk and the two Special Branch Officers.

Russell tried not to fidget in the silence that

followed as the three men read his report. Finally DI Wood began questioning him over the details. It lasted two gruelling hours. Russell went over his story again, offering information on the new crossing they had been shown, the Army movements and the terrorist gangs they had seen moving towards the river. It was suspected that the latter would attempt several imminent boat crossings now that the rains had set in, for the spoors would be instantly obliterated, making detection harder. Russell also repeated the information Sam had felt able to give him, with special emphasis on the details he had acquired about the Russian training camps, the involvement of which, he knew, the powers in Salisbury had long suspected.

At the end of the interview, the Special Branch Officers looked pleased.

"Well, there's one or two new pieces of information here that will be of great value plus confirmation of several other matters that will be extremely useful." Pushing back his chair, DI Wood snapped shut his briefcase and collected his jacket from the back of the chair. Everyone stood up.

"Thank you Patrol Officer Forrester. Your report will be read with interest in Salisbury. Miss Barnard has of course been able to give us some corroborating information and I can tell you that the South Africans are well pleased to have her back without having to contend with any unwelcome propaganda or ransom demands. Well done!"

"Thank you, Sir." Russell looked towards his Superior and saw the forbidding expression on his face.

They all shook hands and the two Special Branch men made to leave. As Andy Thompson passed Russell, he dug him playfully in the ribs.

"Wouldn't be surprised if you get a gong for this, old boy! The story of the gallant policeman rescuing the fair damsel in distress is front page news in Salisbury – and Jo'burg!" He winked and left but as he closed the door behind him, the room fell into an ominous silence.

Makesmith looked long and hard at Russell. He had not bothered to hide his irritation at the aside from Andy Thompson. He prolonged the silence by once more scanning Russell's report. As the long seconds ticked by Russell, much to his own annoyance, felt his cheeks colour as the waiting continued.

Makesmith looked askance at Russell. Judging that sufficient time had lapsed for his purpose, he spoke in acerbic, angry tones.

"Your heroics may be going down well with the newspapers and other riff-raff in Salisbury and elsewhere, but it cuts no bloody ice with me! Have you any idea how many man hours were spent – wasted! – looking for you? Do you imagine I enjoy having to write to a mother telling her that her precious son is missing, presumed dead? It's bloody fortunate for your parents' peace of mind that we decided to hold back sending a telegram until we had positive news one way or the other. Did you ever think about the ramifications of your actions? No bloody thought for anyone else....."

The dressing down lasted more than half an hour, and covered everything from Russell's lack of consideration to his appalling negligence in loosing his rifle, Makesmith inferring that Russell had got his priorities wrong in saving the woman instead of the much more useful FN rifle. By the time Makesmith ran out of steam himself, Russell was totally drained, belittled and cut down to below ground level. His cheeks burnt, perspiration made large dark patches appear on his shirt and his legs ached from standing to attention for so long. At last, he finally heard the words that meant his ordeal was nearly over.

"All right. I've had my say. Its now up to Salisbury whether the matter is taken any further but by all accounts Miss Barnard's glowing account of your actions will have saved your career from ignominy – which is just as well, for I doubt that anyone around here would bloody bother!"

Russell knew he had forever blotted his copybook with Makesmith. It would probably mean a transfer.

"No, Sir. I'm sorry to have caused such a rumpus but.."

"Spare me any more buts, Forester! I've had enough feeble excuses to last me for quite a while. We will just have to wait and see what the Officer Commanding recommends."

"Yes, Sir."

There was another long pause as Makesmith sat at his desk and painstakingly sorted through some papers. He looked up.

"Right! Well then, in the meantime, I still have a station to run."

"Yes, Sir."

"Which means that whilst you have been gallivanting across half of Zambia, the rest of us have had to continue doing the more mundane things in life, like taking prisoners to Court. Six days ago we took your old African before the bench. Ah, yes, I see you've finally remembered him! Well, you will be pleased to know that as we were able to assure the Court that a suitable and reliable home had been found for the man, the Magistrate let him off with a Caution, since which time the stupid bugger has been languishing in the cells, eating like a horse, waiting for someone to have the time to take him up to Franie Coetzee's place. I think as it was your bright idea in the first place, it should be your responsibility to see him safely delivered there this afternoon."

Russell looked beyond his Superior's shoulder to the window where the panes of glass were being pounded by a hail storm. His heart sank.

"Yes, Sir."

"Now, regarding your stupidity in loosing your rifle." Russell inwardly groaned. Surely the old man wasn't going to have another go. "Have you filled in the necessary forms?"

"Yes, Sir. They're on my desk."

"Well, they're no bloody use to anyone out there are they! Go and fetch them."

Russell returned, placing a sizable wad of official forms on the large hardwood desk.

Makesmith first checked, initialled then applied his stamp to the papers before flinging them into his 'Out' tray. He leaned back in his chair, arms in front of his expanding waist line, flexing his fingers.

"All right. Once you have deposited the old man with Franie, I suggest you take three days off. Go up to Kariba or anywhere that's out of my damn sight. I want you back on duty Friday morning, ready to go out on another foot patrol, by which time the Commissioner might just be inclined to trust you with a new rifle. That's it. Now bugger off!"

"Sir!"

Russell left the room, relieved that the worst morning of his police career was over. Even the bawlings out he had received at Training Depot – and he had had plenty of those – paled into insignificance compared to Makesmith's oration. He returned to the mess, sharing a quick drink with Andy Thompson and John Wood before eating a hurried meal. He went to his room, changed out of his uniform into civilian shirt, shorts and casual shoes before packing a few extra items in an overnight bag. Down at the Station cells he collected the old African, seating him in the rear of the Landrover. As Sergeant Nero climbed in the front passenger seat they set off for Franie Coetzee's farm, stopping once at the Motel at Makuti to buy some bottles of beer and a local brew of moonshine tinted with brown dye that passed in the days of sanctions as whisky.

....

Lisa drove the hired car along the straight tarmac road towards Chirundu, squinting through the windscreen as the wipers endeavoured to cope with the heavy rain. The last time she had travelled down this road she had been blissfully unaware of the tragic events about to take place and had innocently enjoyed watching the lush farm lands merge into bush. Today, older, wiser, she sat with white knuckles gripping the steering wheel, her eyes scanning the roadside in a constant nervous motion. She had firmly told herself in the safety of the hotel room that she could handle the journey to Chirundu but an almost overwhelming anxiety had begun to take over her body and mind as soon as the car had left the suburbs of Salisbury and she was alone with the bush. With each mile covered, the past all too vividly returned to haunt her.

It had been an exhausting and confusing thirty six hours of constant questioning by the Police, the South African Embassy and the Media. She longed for a moment's peace to give herself time to catch up with the fast changes that were taking place as much in her own mind as anywhere else. Still emotionally with Dume, Seki and Sam, she had recoiled in distaste at the conceited, boorish behaviour of her fellow South Africans. It triggered off a train of thought about her attitude to the question of apartheid. It would be tremendously risky to speak out against the main stream and she wasn't yet sure whether she had the courage to do so but the idea was forming that she had at last found a cause worthy of her talent. But it was too soon to make a commitment. Her mind was still confused by the events she had endured and she missed Russell. He was the only person who could possibly understand and share her feelings of displacement. Her bosses in Jo'burg had wanted to fly her back immediately, to capitalise on the story whilst it was still hot news but she had held out, insisting on having two days rest. She needed to see Russell.

She felt the sense of relief sweep through her as she approached the comparative safety of the neat whitewashed Station. It was mixed with pleasurable anticipation at being able to see Russell again but as she parked the car she was met by a forbidding, stern faced Member in Charge.

Lisa, pretty in cool cotton, extended a smile and a hand to Makesmith.

"Good afternoon. I'm Lisa Barnard and..." Her voice trailed off as she sensed the hostility.

Makesmith did not take the proffered hand but instead gave a curt nod of acknowledgement.

"Yes, I know who you are. What can we do for you?"

Lisa let her hand fall back to her side. This was not the welcome she had expected. She decided to try again, apologising for her unexpected arrival.

"I'm sorry to call like this, but I was whisked back to Salisbury before I had the opportunity to personally thank Russ..." she saw Makesmith's face turn as dark as the sky above them, "...I mean Patrol Officer Forester, for all that he did for me. I'm due back in Jo'burg so this is my only chance to thank him face to face. Is it possible to see him, if only for a few minutes? I don't want to take up any more of your time than is necessary."

Her sweetest smile was wasted on Makesmith who considered any woman visitor an unwanted intrusion to his all male world but this woman in particular, reminding everyone of his young subordinate's escapade, was even more unwelcome than most. The reply was unyielding, bordering on downright rude.

"Well, I'm extremely sorry, Miss Barnard, but it seems you have had a wasted journey. Had we known you were coming...." Makesmith shrugged. "....As it is, I'm afraid you've just missed him. Patrol Officer Forester is away from the Station on police business and is not expected back for three days."

Lisa eyed Makesmith, trying to decide whether he was telling the truth or just being plain obstructive. Either way, it was obvious she was not going to get the chance to see Russell. A wave of bitter disappointment welled up inside her but determined not to let Makesmith see her distress, she bade the Member in Charge a curt goodbye and got back into the car. Hands on the wheel, she sat staring straight in front of her as she fought off the tears of frustration. She didn't feel safe out here without Russell's protective arm but there was obviously no way she could wait for him to return. She turned the ignition key and keeping her head up and her eyes looking straight ahead, drove out of the Station forecourt back on the road towards the cloud enshrouded escarpment and distant Salisbury.

....

The journey down to the Coetzee farm went smoothly until they turned off the tarmac onto the dirt farm road. The rains had already taken their toll on the graded track, making large muddy ruts and potholes at will. Russell's sour mood suited the challenge of driving in such testing conditions. He drove the Landrover tight lipped with concentration and expertly dodged the worst of the hazards as they bumped and slid at high speed. It helped to ease the frustration within him so he closed his ears to the pitiful wails of 'Please Sah, Please Sah, remember I have a wife and children to think of' that were coming from the anguished Sergeant Nero seated beside him and put his foot down on the accelerator pedal.

The car came to a slithering halt in front of the large inviting house, the passengers only too glad to have the vehicle stationary at last. Russell got out of the car, stretched then leaned over and pipped the horn. He made a supreme effort to put a smile on his face.

Franie appeared from out of one of the barns, wiping his hands on an oily rag as he greeted Russell.

"Ah, you've caused the rain to stop. Good fellow. I see you've brought our little friend to join us."

"Hello, Franie. Yes, this is our geriatric orphan!"

Franie greeted the old man warmly and called out to a middle aged African woman standing shyly in the doorway at the side of the house.

"I'll just see the old boy sorted out and then we can have a chat."

Within ten minutes he had returned.

"Aha, I see you have brought some of the necessities of life with you!"

Russell reached into the back of the Landrover and took out the beer and whisky.

"Good, good. Come inside. Stay for Dinner? There's a spare bed."

Although Russell would normally have welcomed an evening in Franie's enjoyable company, today he was in no mood to be sociable. He lied.

"Err, no. Sorry, I know I said I'd try but I'm under somewhat of a cloud with Makesmith at the moment and he's determined I should make up for lost time."

"Ah, yes, we've been hearing about your adventures. Quite the hero you've turned out to be!"

Russell winced as Franie let out a bellowing laugh.

"So your Superior's none too happy about it. Can't say that surprises me. So what exactly did you get up to?"

"I'm not suppose to say anything at the moment, Franie. Maybe next time, if thats all right."

"Fair enough. Fair enough. I like something to look forward to. You've got time for a beer, though?"

"Sure."

"Send your Sergeant round the back. Susie will take care of him."

The two men drank straight out of the dumpies, sitting companionably on the wide stoep to admire the view of the rolling hills that led up to the Zambesi Escarpment. The rain had left dark storm clouds to mix with the watery late afternoon sun and a clarity in the air made the onlookers feel as if they could touch the far horizon.

"Beautiful, isn't it."

"Yes it is but listen, Franie, whilst I'm here, you ought to know we have reason to believe that terrorist gangs are about to come over in large numbers."

"Yes, I heard on the radio that things have been a bit hot lately, helped in no small way by you!" Again Franie laughed at Russell's discomfiture.

"Seriously Franie, you should start taking precautions."

"What! Me?" Seeing the genuine concern on Russell's face, Franie stood up and walked into his house. "I want you to see something."

Russell could hear him in the hallway. There was the sound of a drawer opening and closing then Franie reappeared with a crumpled piece of paper in his hand.

"Read this. It was pinned to the door of one of my tobacco barns a while back." Russell took the piece of paper that looked like it had been torn from a school exercise book. It was addressed to Mr. Coetzee and was from 'Comrade Colonel Tembo', Regional ZAPU Commander. It stated that because Franie was known to treat his African labour force well, he would not be a target of the Freedom Fighters and therefore it would not be necessary for him to fortify his house.

Russell whistled. What made the note plausible for him was the fact that he knew most of the farmers so far attacked had records of ill-treatment of black labourers.

"Has anyone else seen this?"

"What? You mean officialdom? Hell, no. They'd probably laugh, screw it up and tell me it was a load of old rubbish, but I believe it, Russell. My Foreman says its genuine and I'm going to put my trust in it."

"Well, I admire you Franie, and I hope you're proved right. Nevertheless, a little bit of extra vigilance never hurt anyone."

"Point taken."

Russell finished his beer and bade farewell. He called for Sergeant Nero and was about to climb into the Landrover when the old African shuffled up to him. He clapped his hands together and through a toothless grin thanked Russell.

"Datenda Mambo, Datenda Mambo." he repeated until Russell, trying to hide his embarrassment covered his confusion by gruffly saying that the man should take note that he was already under Caution and any further mis-conduct would result in being sent to prison. He settled himself in the driver's seat, switched on the engine and started the long drive back.

He had already made up his mind to stay the night at the Makuti Motel, organising his room as he brought the beer and whisky earlier in the day. From there he would try to hitch-hike a lift to Kariba the following day. As they arrived at the Motel, he pulled up next to the only other vehicle in the car park.

Sergeant Nero happily took over the driver's seat and after Russell had picked up his bag from the back, accelerated away in the direction of Chirundu Station.

Russell raised a curious eyebrow as he walked past the other vehicle. It was a new Datsun, a rare sight in the days of sanctions. He shrugged. Maybe the owner would be in the bar.

He ambled into the lounge bar but it was empty save for the bar attendant who was idly polishing some glasses. He flashed a wide smile at the sight of Russell.

"Beer, Sah?"

"Yes, thanks."

Russell sat morosely on the bar stool, looking at the glass of beer in front of him. He lit a cigarette and blew out the smoke. How many times on the trek through Zambia had he fantasied about a moment like this? But now that it was here, it did nothing to satisfy him. He thought of Lisa. Was she back in South Africa? Probably. Soaking up the limelight? Well, good for her. But he missed her. Hell, they had not even had the chance to say goodbye. He wanted to talk about Sam, about the treasure, it was all too much to keep silent about, yet without her, he could say nothing.

He swivelled the dregs of his beer around his glass, drained it down in one gulp and waved the empty glass to signal a re-fill.

The bar man instantly brought a fresh beer but as he placed the bottle in front of Russell, a few coins rattled across the bar top. From behind him he heard a sultry voice.

"I'll pay for the beer. I owe this gentleman a drink." Before he could turn round, an hotel key joined the coins on the bar.

"I went up to Chirundu but you weren't there. Nice boss you have, by the way. You never mentioned what a truly charming man he was."

Russell allowed a lazy smile to spread across his face as he pictured Makesmith's reaction to Lisa's arrival.

"I started back to Salisbury but by the time I got as far as Makuti and the Motel, I decided it was too late to go all the way back tonight. As I signed the Register, I thought I recognised a familiar name and asked about you."

Sensual perfume wafted tantalisingly into his nostrils as an elegant arm coiled round his neck. His whole body tensed with excitement as her body touched his back and a long, slender finger gently traced itself across his cheek.

"Mmm, rather like you without a beard – and guess what?"

Russell was alive with anticipation. Soft strands of hair brushed against his face as she bent down and whispered in his ear.

"The Proprietor insists we have the honeymoon suite."